OTHER WORKS by JESSICA DALE

The Unintended Consequences Trilogy

(sweet romance/heart-pounding suspense)

PAYBACK

BACKLASH

BACKFIRE

The Binding Love Duet

(steamy romance/spine-tingling suspense)

Binding Vows

Binding Choice

Bartered Innocence, A Romantic Thriller

(a steamy stand-alone)

~~

SERIES by KASSANDRA LAMB

The Kate Huntington Mysteries

Psychotherapist Kate Huntington helps others cope with trauma, but she has led a charmed life... until a killer rips it apart. (10 novels, 4 Kate on Vacation novellas)

The Marcia Banks and Buddy Cozy Mysteries

Marcia Banks trains service dogs for veterans, and solves crimes on the side, with the help of her Black Lab, Buddy. (13 novels/novellas)

The C.o.P. on the Scene Mysteries

Eight days into her new job as Chief of Police in a small Florida city, Judith Anderson finds herself one step behind a serial killer. (spinoff from the Kate Huntington series; 4 stories–more to come)

BACKFIRE

An Unintended Consequences
Romantic Suspense
JESSICA DALE

a misterio press publication

CHAPTER ONE

Mary

I think I made a mistake when I told James about the dating service.

My friends have been so protective ever since my husband left me. I've appreciated their concern, but it can rankle sometimes.

And James has been the worst and the best of my friends. He's been there in every way he could—more than the others, to tell the truth. But he's also been...it's hard to describe.

Two of our closest friends, Annaleise and her husband Charles were murdered last fall. James found the bodies. Their deaths hit all of us hard, of course, but they've affected him in ways I don't think he's realized.

Now he's trying to talk me out of meeting in person with the most promising guy I've found through the dating service.

Ignoring James's latest text, I went into my bedroom to get ready for the date.

The. Date. I sucked in air and let it out slowly. My first date in eight years—six years of marriage to a bastard and almost two years of recovering from him.

I tamed my long blonde hair into a French braid and applied my makeup. Then I took the little black dress out of my closet. I'd bought it last week. Prior to that, I hadn't owned a little black dress in years.

Four years into my marriage, I'd gone from a four to a six in dress size. You would've thought I'd gained fifty pounds.

My ex wouldn't let me live it down— I was fat, a tubbo, the insults got worse over time. Along with a lot of other things.

I shook my head to clear it, then carefully pulled the dress on, trying not to dislodge my hair nor smear my makeup.

At first, all I saw in the full-length mirror on my closet door were the rolls of pudge. I narrowed my eyes, as Annaleise had taught me to, pointing out that people rarely examine our appearance half as intently as we do ourselves. She was right. Slightly out of focus, I looked okay. More than okay.

You go, girl! Annaleise's voice, echoing faintly in my head. I smiled.

X was waiting for me outside the restaurant, as we'd arranged. He wore a white carnation in his lapel.

The fact that he wouldn't give a name, only the letter X, was the only thing that put me off about him. Everything else about his profile sounded ideal. He'd promised he would explain about the "weird nomenclature" after we'd gotten to know each other some more.

It was an odd first date. We'd already "talked" a lot on the dating service's internal email app—about everything from favorite books and songs to what was on our bucket lists. But we hadn't gotten much into more personal topics.

So I felt I knew him, but I didn't...not completely. I had told myself I was going to take this slow.

After ordering our food, we exchanged some basic background information on our families and such. Nothing all that deep. He could hate his mother for all I knew, but who admits to such things on a first date?

He was quite sweet, and attractive in a generic way. Not movie-star handsome, but he had a pleasant face. Dark curly hair that flopped onto his forehead now and again, a slender nose, firm chin. He was slightly taller than average and had a medium build. He could probably blend in anywhere he went.

His eyes were his best feature, a soft brown, full of kindness, surrounded by dark lashes.

Not that I cared all that much what he looked like. Appearance wasn't high on my criteria list. But my group of friends included several stage actors, James among them. Their discussion of the physical attributes of their fellow thespians had made me more observant of such things.

James contended that appearance affected people's emotional reactions to someone in subtle ways. He'd described how body language interplayed with physical characteristics to set a certain mood in a scene, even before the actors opened their mouths.

X was relaxed now, but he'd been kind of tense when we'd first greeted each other. I was too, of course. This was a blind date of sorts. And we didn't even have some mutual friend telling us they knew we'd hit it off.

As we lingered over dessert, I got up the nerve to ask, "So, are you going to tell me at least your first name?"

He smiled and the dimple I'd noticed earlier made another appearance—the slightest indentation in his left cheek. It gave him a certain boyish charm.

My chest warmed, along with my cheeks. "You don't have to if you don't want to."

"The problem is," he said, "my name is very unusual, and I have, shall we say, some notoriety. There's a very good reason why I need to keep a low profile right now." He paused, took a deep breath. "I didn't want to lie to you and give a false name, so I figured just using my initial for a while would be better."

I felt a bit queasy. All that sounded like it should be reasonable but...

"If you're keeping a low profile, why are you on a dating site at all?"

"Oh well, I'd joined the site long before the reason for the low profile came up. I'd forgotten all about it, hadn't been active on there in a while. Then I remembered and went in to delete my info, and saw your response to it. I set it to inactive and took down my picture. You're the only one who can communicate with me there now."

"I'd wondered what had happened to your photo," I said, still trying to decide if I believed all this. When you've been married to an abusive man, you develop a healthy distrust of surface charm.

We finished our dessert, and X paid the tab. Outside, I pulled my black lace shawl snug around my shoulders. The summer evening had turned cool.

"Can I see you home?" he asked.

I smiled up at him. "Not this time."

He smiled back, his body still at ease. "So, you're willing to go out with me again?"

"Yes, I'd like that."

"Good. I'll call you. And maybe next time I'll tell you my name."

"And maybe next time," I said in a flirtatious voice, "I'll let you see me home."

His smile turned into a grin. He held up his phone. "I'll get you an Uber."

I shook my head and pulled my phone from my evening bag. "I'll call one for myself."

We stood next to each other on the sidewalk, both tapping info into our phones. Then we looked up at the same moment. He chuckled softly. "Modern dating, eh?"

He pocketed his phone and took a step closer. "While we're waiting, may I kiss you goodnight?"

I tilted my head to one side, debating. I'd promised myself I'd go slow. I didn't want to fall for this guy before I truly knew him, as I had with Nick, my ex.

But the kiss would be time-limited, since the Ubers were on their way.

"I think that would be nice," I said.

His lips brushed mine, soft and dry. Then he increased the pressure.

Warmth spread through me. He gently wrapped his arms around me.

A tingling started in my chest and moved downward. Without realizing I was doing it, I let my lips drift apart.

He took that as an invitation and deepened the kiss. The woodsy undertones of his aftershave enveloped me.

The warmth intensified, shot down through my core. Parts of my body that had been dormant for a long time were waking up. A deep, hollow longing built in my gut, and a slow, hot throbbing below there. I wanted this man!

Slow down! You promised yourself.

The thought that he might think me a slut finally made me break the kiss. I was gasping a little.

A throat clearing nearby. Our heads jerked toward the sound.

A car was now parked at the curb beside us, a young woman in a denim jacket leaning against the driver's door and staring at us over the roof. "You know, you can do that in my backseat if you like. I promise not to watch."

X chuckled, a low rumble in his chest, which was still pressed against mine. He stepped back, and I felt quite chilled.

He pulled out his phone again and glanced at it. "Must be yours," he said. "My driver's name is Hugo and he looks like a linebacker."

I let out a giggle, and felt my cheeks warming.

He smiled down at me, his eyes sparkling with humor. Opening the back door, he handed me into the car, then leaned in through the open door and kissed me chastely on my cheek. "Sleep tight," he whispered.

His woodsy aftershave kept me company on the ride home.

———◦———

James

A phone ringing in the middle of the night never bodes well. My heart was pounding by the time I'd fumbled it off my nightstand.

I glanced at the other side of my bed. Carrie was gone. She always went home at some point during the night, unwilling to have her teenage son find her missing in the morning. He, of course, knew what was going on. We lived next door to each other. But Carrie still felt she should maintain some semblance of propriety.

The screen read *Mary*. A lump of dread formed in my stomach. I answered the call.

Sobbing.

"Mary?"

More sobs.

My throat tightened. "Mare, talk to me."

The sobs shifted, sounded more like dry heaves. Finally she said, "You were right, okay!" Her tone was furious. "He's..."

Renewed sobs.

"He's what? Who's he?"

"X. I went out with him tonight. I had a lovely time." Her voice was still choked with tears, but no longer as angry. "He was the perfect gentleman. And then–" She broke off abruptly, crying harder again.

I was sitting up on the side of the bed by now. "Mary, tell me what happened?"

"He broke into my place," she yelled, "and raped me."

CHAPTER TWO

James

"Oh my God! Did you call the police?"

"No," Mary said. "I'm...not ready to deal with that yet."

I pulled on my jeans one-handed. "I'm on my way."

"James, you're almost two hours away."

What did that mean? Did she not want me to come?

"You want me to call someone else? Maybe Sharon and Patrick. Or Todd." All mutual friends, although we hadn't been as close since Annaleise had....

"Nooo." Mary's wail interrupted that train of thought.

I slipped my feet, sockless, into my loafers. "I'll drive fast."

"Don't speed," she shrieked into my ear.

"I won't," I lied. Grabbing up a tee shirt, I ran for the stairs.

"I couldn't bear it if something happened to you because of me."

"I'll drive carefully. Stay on the line with me, Mare. We'll keep each other company."

"That would be good. I need to stay awake."

"Why?" Sleep would probably be the best thing for her, a respite from the horror for a while.

"I'm sitting at my kitchen table," she said, "my biggest butcher knife in my hand."

"Why don't you try to lie down, on the couch maybe?"
"I can't. The bastard broke the lock on my door."

With no traffic in the middle of the night, I got there in an hour and twenty-five minutes. I'd stopped only briefly, to whiz off the side of the highway into a dark ravine below—praying I wasn't peeing on someone's back deck.

Mary had stopped answering my questions about a half hour before I arrived. I hoped that meant she'd found some solace in sleep.

Her apartment door was indeed hanging ajar. Breaking in like that, he had to have made some noise. Why hadn't the neighbors called the police?

I slipped quietly into the apartment. Mary *had* fallen asleep, head on her crossed arms on the kitchen table. Her phone was held limply in one hand, the other had relaxed. But the knife she'd described lay next to it.

I put my hand on her shoulder and gently shook it.

She roared out of her chair and almost gutted me.

Mary

One minute, he was on top of me, his ski-masked face hovering inches from mine. His hot breath seared my skin.

And those brown eyes, now hard as marbles, boring into me. Those beautiful eyes I'd admired all evening, and had thought seemed so kind.

Then we were in the kitchen and he was grabbing me. I leaped up and lunged.

James jumped backward, my knife missing his stomach by a half inch, at best.

Horror filled me. I dropped the knife and my hands flew to my mouth. "Oh no! I'm so sorry."

And then I was sobbing in James's arms.

When the sobs had subsided to sniffles, he sat me back down in my chair. He picked up the butcher knife and tossed it in the sink. Sitting down across from me, he took one of my hands. "Tell me what you can?"

I hiccuped and took a deep breath. I told him about the date, the only off part being X's unwillingness to give me his name.

"That's what he calls himself—just X?" James asked.

I nodded and repeated X's mumbo-jumbo about having to keep a low profile. It sounded even less convincing than it had earlier.

"Do you want to talk about the rest of it?" James asked gently.

I shook my head. "I think I'm ready to deal with the police. I'd rather not repeat it twice."

"Do you want to go to the hospital, get a rape kit done?"

I nodded again, even though that was actually the last thing I wanted to do. But my parents had raised me to be a responsible person.

Good old Mary Reliable, always doing what she was supposed to do.

"Okay, I'll take you," James said, "and after, you're coming to Virginia. Does this X know anything about me?"

"I mentioned we were good friends. He said he'd heard of you." I took a deep breath. It came out on a shudder. "I didn't tell him about your house in Virginia, though."

"Then that's the safest place for you," James said, his voice firm.

Part of me wanted to argue. I glanced at the red-checked curtains I'd pulled tight over my kitchen window, as if X could see into my third-floor walk-up. It would be daylight soon, and I was exhausted. But I couldn't stay here, not with a busted lock on the apartment door.

I nodded yet again and rose from the table. The thought of facing the bedroom, where he'd attacked me, stopped me cold. "Could you pack a bag for me, my toiletries and a couple changes of clothes?"

"Sure," James said and stood. He patted my shoulder as he walked past me, pretending not to notice when I flinched.

James

Gathering a platonic female friend's belongings wasn't a particularly comfortable process. But I wasn't about to wimp out on Mary. She was dealing with a lot worse than having to handle someone else's underwear.

I tried a tactic that sometimes worked with stage jitters before a performance. I focused on a mental task to distract myself. Mary'd said X had implied it was the first initial of his given name. What male names did I know that began with X?

I could only think of two—Xavier and Xander. I'd known a Xavier in college, in the drama club. His nickname had been Avi. I'd lost track of him after graduation.

It had worked. Recalling my college days had gotten me past the embarrassing moments of tossing panties and bras into Mary's pink duffle bag.

Mary had changed her mind about calling the police. The nurse at the hospital said she could take the photos and samples she needed—swabs and fingernail clippings and such—and Mary could complete the rest of the interview that went with the rape kit later.

While I waited for her, I called her office to tell her lawyer boss that she wouldn't be coming in today. It was still quite early and I'd expected to get voicemail, but someone picked up.

"Larry Bevans."

"Uh, this is James Fitzgerald. I'm calling in for Mary Hanson. She won't be able to come to work today."

"Is she okay? What happened?"

"Um..." I hated to flat out lie to a lawyer. "She had a rough night."

"Is she sick?"

"Yeah. Upset stomach, off and on, all night." That wasn't a total lie. No doubt, Mary had felt queasy more than once in the last few hours.

"Is it serious?"

"No, I don't think so. Probably a bug she picked up." Okay, that was a lie, but I wasn't going to share Mary's business with anyone, not even her boss of several years.

"Well, tell her to take as much time as she needs." His voice sounded relieved.

"I will. Thank you, sir." I disconnected.

Once we were back in my car and headed toward Virginia, I told Mary about my conversation with her boss. She nodded.

"Are you sure about not calling the police?" I asked.

"No. But I just can't handle–" Mary stopped abruptly, turned her head toward the passenger window. I detected a soft sniffling sound.

Then she blew out a sigh. "I'm afraid they won't believe me. They'll say it was consensual and I'm only saying it's rape now because..." She trailed off.

"Why would they say that?" I kept my words soft.

"Because I went out with him." Her voice was hard—a tone I'd rarely heard from gentle Mary.

"That doesn't mean he had the right to break into your place later and–"

"I know that," she interrupted angrily, "but you know how some people can be about rape."

Yes, I knew a thing or two about that, since my biological father was a rapist.

Mary looked over at me, her mouth open and eyes wide. "Oh, James, I'm sorry. I wasn't thinking."

I shrugged it off. "No worries. And I get how you might not want to deal with some cop's skepticism right now." I let the thought hang there, implying that she might change her mind later.

After a moment, I asked, "Why are you so sure it was X? You said he was wearing a ski mask."

She stared out the side window again. "Because he said some things. Talked about stuff I'd told X."

"That you told him last night?" I was wondering if maybe someone at the restaurant had been eavesdropping.

"No. Stuff I told him in messages, when we'd chatted on the dating service's app."

"How secure is that likely to be?" I asked.

She shrugged. "They claim the chat rooms are totally private."

"Can you tell me what things he said?...I mean, you don't have to if..."

She shook her head slightly. "We got to talking one day on there about our exes. His old girlfriend, and my husband. I told him how Nick had always tried to tear me down. I gave him some specific examples. He, um..." She bit her lower lip, then cleared her throat. "He repeated them back to me while he was attacking me."

I nodded. It sounded like the same guy to me.

We rode in silence for a while. Mary had closed her eyes. I hoped she was getting some sleep.

Suddenly, she bolted upright. "I was such a fool."

"What do you mean?"

She sighed, shook her head.

"Come on, Mare, you can't tease me like that." I tried for a light tone, but I wasn't sure I'd pulled it off.

"He asked to see me home. I told him no, and he offered to call an Uber for me."

"You didn't give him–"

"No," she cut me off. "I'm not that stupid. I called one for myself. Mine came first and we said good night." She paused, turned her head away, toward her side window. "But his Uber probably came right after that. He could've easily followed me home."

Several responses—that might or might not make her feel better—ran through my mind. They all sounded lame.

So I opted not to say anything.

After a minute, she closed her eyes again and leaned her head back against the headrest.

The crunch of gravel under my Mustang's wheels had her opening her eyes. She blinked, then sat up straighter in the passenger seat.

"You know, this will be the first time I've stayed here overnight since..." She trailed off.

But she didn't need to finish the sentence. ...*since Annaleise and Charles had been killed in my house.*

She'd been here a few times, but only for the day. One time, it had gotten late and she'd sacked out on Carrie's sofa rather than sleep in my house. "With the ghosts," she'd said.

She didn't know how close that was to the truth.

I carried her duffle bag inside. Mary paused in the living room, looking around.

I felt a familiar warmth envelop me. A soft "Oh my!" breathed into my ear, the tone sad and worried both.

Mary visibly relaxed. My guess was she could feel the warmth but hadn't heard the words.

"The energy, it's good," she said. "Did you have an exorcism done or something?"

"Or something," I said.

I had set her duffle bag on the floor. Now I leaned down to pick it up again.

She grabbed the other handle. "I can get it."

I mock wrestled her for it, before letting go. "Okay, go ahead and deprive me of the opportunity to be a gentleman."

Mary actually gave me a small smile.

Wind chimes tinkled in a nonexistent breeze.

"What was that?" Mary's head jerked around again, anxiety back on her face.

"Old house. It makes noises as it settles at night." Although it was past dawn at this point.

Don't mess with her right now, I said inside my head.

The tinkling of wind chimes again.

Mary didn't react. Only *I* had heard Annaleise's response that time.

CHAPTER THREE

James

I got Mary settled in the guest room upstairs, praying she would be able to get some rest.

But I had more important things to do than sleep. I got some coffee brewing, then went to my dining room table—my *de facto* desk—and brought up the dating service on my laptop. I'd already tried calling the phone number X had given Mary. It went straight to voicemail, with a mechanical voice inviting me to leave a message. I did not do so.

My coffee maker beeped softly, just as I located the words *Contact Us*, down at the bottom of the home page. Of course there was no phone number, only a contact form behind the link.

I got up to fetch a mug as I contemplated how to phrase the message. Sipping coffee, I decided to pretend to be a cop, without ever saying that I was.

I sat back down at the computer. With caffeine now zinging through my system, my fingers flew over the keyboard.

Hello,

My name is James Fitzgerald. I am investigating a possible felony assault by one of your customers, perpetrated upon another of your customers.

We require contact information for a male customer who uses X as his screen name.

Your cooperation will be noted.

J. Fitzgerald

The website called their participants *clients*, but I had intentionally not used that word. It implied dating service-client confidentiality, and I doubted there was such a thing.

On to the next task. I called a locksmith's emergency number and arranged to have Mary's door fixed, the frame reinforced, and the lock replaced. I asked him to add an additional deadbolt lock.

When I glanced back at my email inbox, there was already a response from the dating service. Who the heck was working at this hour of the morning?

We're very sorry but we cannot reveal private information about our clients.

Did they have some bot set up to send that out if certain words showed up in a message?

I typed: *A court order could be procured.*

Well it could be—by some cop out there, if Mary was willing to call them.

But it would be to your advantage to save us that time and cooperate, so that it doesn't give the appearance of aiding and abetting a felony. Please call me to discuss this further.

I added my cell number and hit send.

I stared at my phone for a moment, now regretting the cup of coffee. If I couldn't contact this mysterious X, then I should be getting some sleep.

I texted Carrie, knowing she wouldn't see it until she woke up. She muted her phone at night. But she was an early riser, so I'd have only a few hours to wait.

Something happened to Mary. I went to DC and got her, brought her back here. Call when you get this. J

I crossed my arms on the table and put my head down to rest my eyes, while waiting for a call from the dating service or Carrie, whichever happened first.

———◦———

Carrie

First cup of tea in hand, I stepped out onto my front porch, pulling my heavy, shawl-collared sweater around me.

It was the color of oatmeal and had gone better with my hair when I'd been dying it blonde. Not as flattering with my natural auburn color, but it was warm.

The calendar might say early June—and it would get up to around eighty or more by noon—but the mornings here were still chilly. I filled my lungs with the cool air and smiled.

It had been an unusually dry spring, but the world was finally turning green. The poppy seeds I'd scattered in the field in front of my house had done their thing. Now dabs of red, yellow and orange peeked between emerald blades of grass. A backdrop of woods, a darker green, separated James's and my houses from the country road a quarter mile away.

I'd come here originally to hide from my abusive husband, but I'd fallen in love with the rolling hills of northwestern Virginia. As well as with my handsome next-door neighbor.

Letting out a contented sigh, I went back inside to check my phone and see if James was up yet.

The pleasant feelings induced by the lovely morning fled as I read his text. What had happened to Mary?

I grabbed my key to his house from the key rack on the kitchen wall and headed next door.

Once on the wide veranda across the front of his house, I fingered the key in my sweater's pocket. Should I knock or just let myself in?

I didn't want to wake James and/or Mary if they were sleeping—a good possibility at this hour, especially since it sounded like they'd been up half the night. It was close to two hours, one way, to DC.

I stepped over to the kitchen window and peeked in. James had his head down on his arms on the table. Was he asleep?

While debating if I should wake him, I enjoyed the view. Damn, his lean body looked good, in a snug t-shirt and jeans. Dark, slightly wavy hair draped over his tanned, muscular arms.

Suddenly, he jolted upright. Muttering to himself, he glanced my way.

He gave me a small smile and headed out of the room.

I met him at the front door, but instead of inviting me in, he stepped out and gently closed the door behind him.

"Sorry I woke you," I said.

"You didn't. Annaleise did."

Is that who you were talking to?"

He nodded and took my hand.

"Aren't you cold without a jacket?" I asked.

He led me toward the wooden porch swing he'd installed a few weeks ago. "You can snuggle next to me and keep me warm."

We sat and I curled up in the circle of his arm. "So, what happened to Mary?"

"Brace yourself. It's not pretty."

I was glad for the warning when he explained the events of the previous night, ending with, "Mary didn't want to deal with the police, and I told her I'd respect that. So I'm trying to find out who this X is myself."

I stiffened.

He quickly squeezed my shoulders. "Don't worry. It's only some computer research and trying to get the dating service to give me his contact info. Once I have some sense of who or where he is, I'll try again to get Mary to bring in the police."

He sighed. "I think I need to tell her about Annaleise, so she doesn't end up jumping out of her skin if she hears her again. Last night, she seemed to hear the wind chimes."

"Or," I said, "we could try to convey to Annaleise what's happened, so she's more careful around Mary."

"I think she already has a pretty good idea. She whispered 'oh my!' in my ear last night, when we first got here."

"You think she can read minds?"

James shrugged. "Maybe, or at least she can read our emotions pretty good. She picked up right away that Mary was a mess."

His jeans pocket vibrated against my thigh. James swung his arm over my head to dig his phone out. Staring at the screen, he said, "I gotta take this. It's the dating service." He swallowed hard.

I nodded.

"Hello." He listened for a moment, then, "Sir, that isn't acceptable." His voice had a sharp edge. "I have a young woman who's been sexually assaulted. One of your, quote, 'clients' as well."

A pause as he listened again. "Sir, not only would you be impeding an investigation, but you would be setting yourself up for a lawsuit. This young woman, in my opinion, would have a strong civil case if your refusal to give out information kept her from getting justice and a sense of safety, knowing her assailant was locked up."

I gave James an encouraging smile, having figured out what he was doing—trying to sound official without crossing over into flat-out impersonation of a cop.

The furrows on his forehead deepened. "Okay, let's try a different approach. As I understand it, there's some internal way that your clients communicate with each other. If you could give me access to that system, I could contact him. Try to convince him to turn himself in."

A brief pause, then James rattled off his email address. Another pause. "Thank you, sir. Hopefully, I won't need to bother you further."

He disconnected. "Well, it's something. Do you know how to track IP addresses via email accounts?"

"No, but Phillip might." My son would probably be getting up soon. He was an early bird like me, but currently his teenage need for excessive sleep did battle with that predisposition most mornings.

James

I checked on Mary, while Carrie went back to her house to talk to Phillip.

No noises emanated through the door of the guest room. I left a note on the kitchen table, telling her I was next door, then grabbed a light jacket and my laptop. I hiked across the strip of lawn between my house and the old farmhouse that Carrie was remodeling in exchange for cheap rent.

That house had been the bane of my stepfather's existence. He'd renovated my mother's childhood home, giving it a brick facade and a southern-style verandah, but its beauty was diminished, in James Fitzgerald, Sr.'s eyes, by the eyesore next door. He'd attempted multiple times to buy the property but the owner annoyingly resisted his offers and continued to rent the place out to what my parents disdainfully called "poor white trash."

I had never minded my sometimes rowdy neighbors, even if a few of them did consider old cars as appropriate lawn ornaments. Since the two properties were a bit isolated—the only houses at the end of a quarter-mile gravel lane off of a country road—I'd been glad to have someone keeping an eye on the place when I was in DC.

But I much prefer my current neighbor, for obvious reasons.

Carrie's golden retriever, Ginger, greeted me on her porch with a friendly woof and a wagging tail. I rubbed her head and let myself in the front door.

A little zing of joy ran through me each time I found the door unlocked. With her abusive late husband now gone for good, Carrie no longer lived in fear.

"Hello," I called out softly, in case Phillip was still in bed.

"In the kitchen," Carrie called back.

I walked through the still mostly empty living room—a plan was hatching in my brain to take Carrie furniture shopping for her upcoming birthday.

In her small kitchen, Phillip sat in front of his laptop, light brown hair sticking up in all directions. He wore a rumpled white tee shirt and lounge pants—no doubt, he'd slept in them.

"Hey, James," he greeted me, then went back to explaining encryption and VPNs to his mother. I gathered that meant the answer to my question, could someone's IP address be located from their email account, was a resounding no.

Having just turned fifteen, Phillip was beginning to come out of the gangly, uncoordinated stage when teen boys seemed to grow faster than their brains could keep up.

I helped myself to a second cup of coffee from Carrie's coffee maker.

"So, these VNPs," Carrie said, "they hide your location from even your own internet provider?"

"VPNs, Mom." He sighed. "Virtual private networks. Right now anyone trying to track me would think I'm in Germany."

"Can you set up one of them for me?" I asked him.

"Sure." Phillip's blue eyes, so like his mother's, were bright with excitement. He was enjoying being the computer whiz kid, advising the techno-challenged adults.

I opened my laptop on the table, booted it up and slid it over in front of him as he pushed his aside.

"Um, they cost some money."

I dug out my wallet. "How much?"

"Depends on how good you want it to be."

"I'd say, pretty good."

"Then about a hundred bucks for a year."

I handed over my credit card, and he got to work setting up my VPN.

I beckoned Carrie to follow me and went out to the living room, where I proposed the furniture shopping trip.

She was starting to shake her head before I'd even gotten the whole idea out.

"Sweetheart, I want to do this. I've been saving for it."

Her face stubborn, she opened her mouth.

"Done," Phillip called from the kitchen.

Saved by the teenager, I thought. At least, I'd planted the seed.

I hurried in there, and Phillip vacated his chair, gesturing for me to take it.

I called up the dating service site and followed the owner's instructions to get into the private message board. I'd given some thought to what to say. I'd already almost impersonated a cop so might as well pretend to be the dating service management.

Dear Sir, I need to discuss your account with you. Please contact me as soon as possible.

I hesitated, not sure I wanted to give him my real cell phone number. "You still got any of those disposable phones?" I asked Carrie. When she'd been hiding from her abusive husband, she'd changed out her phone monthly, sometimes weekly, depending on how paranoid she was feeling.

She nodded and went to her kitchen junk drawer, dug out a phone and handed it to me.

I added the phone number to the message and signed it with the name of the guy I'd talked to earlier.

I sat back and sighed. "Okay, now we wait."

Carrie reached over and patted my hand. "Why don't you try to get some sleep?"

"Good idea, but what if Mary wakes up?"

"I'll come over with you and hang out in your kitchen, keep an ear out for when she stirs."

"When did Mary get here?" Phillip asked.

Carrie and I exchanged a glance that said *how much should we tell him?* "Last night," I replied.

"She's here for a short visit," his mother quickly added. Apparently the answer to the question was we weren't telling him much.

Phillip looked at his mom, and then me, his expression confused. Then he shrugged.

I almost laughed out loud. I wanted to tell him that adults were a mystery to me as well when I was his age.

But since he probably thought that he *was* almost an adult already, he might not take that the right way.

I tucked my laptop under my arm, and Carrie and I left him to his favorite pastime—playing video games.

A banging noise dragged me out of a sound sleep.

I rolled over and started to pull my pillow over my head, willing to let Carrie deal with whoever it was.

Then I woke up enough to realize it could be X. Maybe he'd figured out how to track my message, despite the VPN. I bolted out of bed, grabbed my jeans but didn't bother to put them on. Bare-chested, I ran downstairs.

More banging as I reached the foot of the steps, but I ran to the kitchen first. I wanted to know where the women were, before I opened the door to a possible rapist.

No one was there. A note propped against the salt shaker said, *We're next door.* The clock on my stove indicated it was after eleven.

I trotted back toward the front entranceway, while trying to pull on my jeans without tripping myself.

I really *need to install a peephole in this door*, I thought for the umpteenth time.

Sucking in air, I yanked the door open, ready to do battle.

A big man in a khaki uniform stood on the porch. Sheriff Joe Wallace.

"Son, I need ya to come into the office," he drawled. "Man there wants to meet ya."

"Who?"

He looked me up and down. "Fella from the DC police. Somethin' about impersonating a law enforcement officer while investigatin' a rape yourself."

My stomach churned.

"Might wanna grab a shirt." Wallace gazed pointedly at my crotch. "And finish gettin' dressed."

My face heated as I zipped my fly.

CHAPTER FOUR

James

Detective Robert Talley, of the DC Metropolitan Police Department, sat stiffly across the conference table from me and the sheriff. His expression and body language said he was not in a good mood.

And apparently being left to cool his heels at the sheriff's department while Wallace came out to my house to fetch me had not improved his disposition one bit.

Talley's tone was derisive as he questioned this action.

Wallace shrugged. "Didn't know for sure the boy would be home," he said in his best small-town-hick-sheriff voice.

I resisted the urge to chuckle. The sheriff loved it when people underestimated him.

I knew he'd had two reasons for leaving Talley behind. One he'd admitted to me—he didn't want the detective upsetting Mary if she was at my house.

He'd cleared his throat and added, "I've had a family member who was assaulted. She was pretty easily spooked for a long time after."

My guess was one of his grown daughters, but I didn't ask for details.

I'd figured out the other reason during the drive to town—the sheriff wanted to grill me on what had happened, *before* he let Talley interrogate me.

I had filled him in on all...well, *most* of what I'd done. I left out the implication that I could get a search warrant for the dating service's records. And I'd repeated several times that I never actually said I was a police officer.

Now, I repeated the whole story to Detective Talley, again leaving out a few details. "I was very careful," I told him, "not to imply that I was a police officer. I just said I was investigating the situation."

Talley grunted. "Oh, I think you implied plenty. And there's the matter of interfering with a crime scene. When I went to Ms. Hanson's apartment, some guy was fixing her door. He said you arranged it. That's how I got your address."

"How did you find out about the assault in the first place?" I asked.

"I'll ask the ques–"

The sheriff interrupted Talley. "Seems the manager of the dating service called to confirm your identity, then reported the assault. He didn't want to be seen as obstructing justice."

Talley shot him a dirty look.

"Great!" I said. "The guy wouldn't give me anything on a potential rapist but he'll reveal the identity of a victim."

"Because he now knew," Talley said with a sneer, "that he was *really* talking to the police."

I couldn't help wondering why this guy was working so hard to track down the victim of a rape that hadn't even been reported by said victim.

I kept that thought to myself and asked instead, "So, can you find this X guy?"

"Thanks to you," Talley said, "he's already shut down his account with the dating service. Now, I need to talk to Ms. Hanson."

I pulled out my phone and called Mary. When she answered, I told her the dating service had reported the crime and a DC detective was in town, wanting to interview her.

A long pause. "I guess. Can you or Carrie stay in the room with me?"

"She says yes," I told Talley, "but only if Carrie or me can stay with her during the interview." I intentionally phrased it a little more firmly than Mary had.

"Who's Carrie?" Talley asked.

"My neighbor."

Wallace arched one of his bushy eyebrows at me. They were sandy-colored, like his hair, both with a hefty amount of gray sprinkled in. "And she's his girlfriend," he told Talley.

Talley's own eyebrows went up. "How many girlfriends do you have?"

"Only one," I said. "Mary and I are platonic friends. We've known each other for years."

Talley grunted again. I took that to mean he didn't really believe in platonic friendship.

Frankly, I didn't give a rat's ass what he believed, as long as he tracked down this X bastard.

⚬

Mary

I was beginning to regret asking that James sit in on the interview. There seemed to be some underlying animosity between him and the DC detective.

The sheriff had come along as well, and his role seemed to be that of mediator.

I felt like the least important person in the room.

Carrie sat beside me at James's dining room table. She was holding my hand and gave it a squeeze.

The same warm feeling I'd had last night enveloped me. *You're important to me.*

Where the H had those words come from?

Carrie? Did she have some kind of telepathic abilities?

She gently shook my hand, bringing me out of my reverie. The detective had asked me another question.

"I'm sorry. What?"

"Why are you so sure the man was the guy you had a date with earlier?" Detective Talley asked again.

"Because he knew things that only X would know."

"Such as?"

I hesitated, heat rising in my cheeks. I really didn't want to get into that. "Things my ex-husband said to me."

The detective gave me a fake shocked look. "You told this stranger you met online about intimate discussions with your husband?"

James opened his mouth.

"No, not intimate stuff," I quickly said, to cut James off. Then I paused, swallowed hard. My stomach was queasy. Good thing I hadn't had anything to eat since last night.

"Mean stuff my ex had said to me. It was in the context of complaining about previous relationships. X was telling me about his demanding ex-girlfriend as well."

The detective nodded, his expression saying loud and clear that he was pretending to believe me.

Suddenly red-hot anger swelled in my chest. I wanted to punch the man. Why would I make this crap up?

"And when you say that your attacker knew these things," the detective seemed to be picking his words carefully, "how did you know that?"

"He repeated those things to me."

"What do you mean?" His voice was more gentle now, but still...

I took a deep breath. "He said, 'Your husband was right. You are a fat pig.' Things like that."

James stirred, opened his mouth again. Carrie gave him a quelling look.

After a couple of beats of silence, Detective Talley rose. "I'll be in touch. If you think of anything else, let me know." He dropped a business card on the table.

Carrie rose and showed him out.

The sheriff lingered.

"Sheriff Wallace," James said, "doesn't it strike you as strange that a big city cop would come all this way to track down the victim of a crime who hasn't even reported that crime yet?"

The sheriff placed his big hands on the table and pushed his bulk up out of his chair. "Yes, son," he said in a drawl, "it strikes me as mighty strange indeed. That's why I tagged along."

He plopped his hat on his head and left the room, without saying another word.

Carrie's voice, unintelligible, from the entranceway, followed by the sheriff's low rumble. Then the front door closed.

I turned to James. "What do you think it means that this detective came to Virginia?"

He shook his head slowly. "I don't know."

My phone buzzed in my pocket, as Carrie returned to the dining room.

I stood and pulled it out, looked at the screen. *Unknown Caller*.

"Should I answer it?"

James held out his hand. I hesitated, but truth be told I was glad for his overprotectiveness right now. I gave him the phone.

"Hello." James's face paled. He stared at me. "It's X."

I felt the blood drain from my own face. Carrie caught me as my knees buckled.

CHAPTER FIVE

James

"Who the hell are you?" I yelled into the phone.

"James? Is that you?" Slight surprise in the man's voice.

"How do you know who I am?" A small, still-sane part of my brain was telling me to calm down. The infuriated-beyond-reason part wasn't listening. "You've got a helluva nerve, you bastard!"

"Look, it wasn't me. I didn't hurt Mary." He sounded choked up. "I'd never hurt her."

"Yeah, right!"

"Please listen to me. You know me—but don't say my name." He was talking fast, his tone a bit frantic. "We went to school together, were in–"

"Avi?"

"Don't say my full name! Please! You could get me killed."

"What the hell is going on?"

"Listen, I'll explain everything. Give me a minute, okay? First, is Mary all right?"

"No, she's not! I mean, physically she's okay, but..."

"I understand. But you gotta believe me, I did *not* do it! I went home and went to bed. Then I'm dragged out of a sound sleep this morning by a call from my handler–"

"Your handler?" I blurted out.

I waved the women into chairs at the table. They sat without taking their eyes off me.

"Yeah. It's a long story," the voice on the phone continued. "Remember how I went out to Hollywood after we graduated?"

"Yes." I sat down myself, trying to process what I was hearing. How the hell could Mary's rapist be my college friend, Xavier?

"Well, I failed as an actor, big time, so I fell back on accounting, my major in school. Eventually, I became the accountant for some of the big-name producers. Nine months ago, I discovered one of them was laundering money for the mob. I turned him in, and now I'm in—well, it's kinda like witness protection—until he goes to trial."

Mary's shell-shocked expression was morphing toward anger. She made a grab for her phone.

I held up a hand. "Repeat all that. I'm putting you on speaker." I did so and laid the phone on the table.

Avi told his story again.

At first, Mary shuddered at the sound of his voice. Then she just stared at the phone. When he fell quiet, she said, "You and James were friends?"

He sighed. "Yes, in college, here in DC. We met in drama club. He knows me as Avi. Like I told you, I'd forgotten about the dating service account. I went in to close it down but you were there, responding to my inquiry from months before." He paused. "Mary, I don't regret getting to know you one bit. Even though it's pissed off my handler big time."

Another sigh. "He didn't know about our date. I'm supposed to stay in my apartment at all times, but I had to see you."

"But why are you back in DC?" I interjected.

"The producer's company is based in New York. That's where the trial will be. I asked to come to DC to wait. I don't know why. I guess I thought it would be good to be someplace familiar. But they won't let me go anywhere." The sound of air being blown out. "I haven't even been able to visit my folks."

"So how'd you slip your leash?" I asked, not sure I believed him.

"They have agents watching my place, but they're looking for someone who's trying to get *in*. It wasn't that hard to get past them to get out. Look, I'm on a throwaway phone, but they're gonna make me get off of it soon. I just had to find out if Mary was okay and let her know it wasn't me who..." A choking sound.

Still not sure I believed him, I said, "The attacker knew things Mary had told you–"

"What things?"

"Stuff Nick said to me," Mary answered before I could stop her.

Damn! I'd been trying to trip Avi up.

"Did you tell anyone about that?" Mary asked.

"No, of course not. Why would I? Hell, *who* would I tell?"

"Hey," I said, "we need to have a way to get in touch with you–"

"Not this number. This phone will be smashed the minute we hang up. I'll figure out a way though. Um, my handler's been talking to the DC cops. He's giving them a sample of my DNA to test. But you gotta release the rape kit to the cops, okay, Mary?"

"Okay," she said in a small voice.

"You'll see it wasn't me, and then... Please I gotta see you again, know you're okay." His voice sounded desperate.

Mary had tears streaming down her face. I jumped in before she could commit to something she might regret later. "We'll see. One step at a time."

"Okay." Voices in the background. "I gotta go."

And he was gone.

We all sat for a few minutes, staring at the phone in stunned silence.

"Now we know why a DC cop drove down here to chase down a crime victim," I finally said.

"What do you mean?" Mary asked.

"Assuming the dating service owner gave the police X's contact info, when Talley tried to find him, it no doubt triggered something in the system and alerted his handlers. Then they sent Talley down here to check you out."

Carrie was nodding her head. "Maybe they were afraid you were working for the mobsters?"

"So," I said, "if we believe Avi that he didn't tell anybody anything you shared with him, could it be Nick who..." I trailed off.

Mary shook her head. "No, he has hazel eyes. This guy's eyes were brown. Besides, I'd know Nick, even with a ski mask on. I know how he carries himself, how he smells."

She stopped, sucked in air. "Besides, there's something I told X, I mean Avi–"

"We can keep calling him X if that's easier for you," I said.

"No, I like Avi. It sounds softer, nicer. I just have to get used to it."

"What else did you tell him?" I asked her.

"Um, about this ceramic doll I have. I didn't have it when I was married to Nick, and I never mentioned it to him. After my mom died, I found it among her things, along with a note explaining its significance. It's a girl doll but it's dressed in a Navy uniform. Her grandfather brought it back as a souvenir from Europe at the end of WWI."

She paused, took another deep breath. "I'd told X, uh, Avi about it. The guy, when he was in my room, he saw it and commented on it. Said something about how it looked exactly like I'd described it."

Carrie and I exchanged a glance. "Maybe," she said in a gentle voice, "it was X after all."

Mary started shaking her head. Then she suddenly stopped and stared at me. "Remember I said I'd recognize Nick's scent?"

"Yeah."

"It *was* X who..." Her face began to crumple. "...who attacked me. I smelled his aftershave." She burst into tears.

CHAPTER SIX

James

I had an audition the next day, for a really good part in a play in DC. I couldn't afford to not go, but I was anxious about leaving Mary alone.

"I'm not a child, James," she protested, when I'd suggested Carrie could come over and stay with her. "I don't need a babysitter."

"Okay, but you call her or go over there if you start feeling anxious or lonely," I said.

She gave me a weak smile. "I'll be fine."

I nodded, even though she didn't look fine at all. She'd visibly aged in the last thirty hours. Her forehead was now marred with worry lines, and she had bags under her eyes. Her long blonde hair, normally her pride and joy, was straggly, and her clothes hung loosely on her slender body.

She looked like a waif, a very unhappy waif.

I left early, allowing time for another stop while in the city. Once on the road, I called Mary's office and asked for an appointment with her boss. Under the guise of asking for a leave of absence for her, I planned to grill him about anyone in the office who might want to do her harm.

It was a long shot, and the rapist being someone from the law firm wouldn't explain the bastard's knowledge of the intimate details she'd shared with X/Avi.

But I wanted it to be someone other than him. He'd sounded so sincere on the phone, and my memories of him were fond ones. I found it hard to believe he'd evolved into a rapist. Or maybe the word should be *devolved*.

I was informed by his assistant that Mary's boss, Mr. Bevans, was in a meeting. She invited me to leave a message, which I did, keeping my reason for wanting to meet with him vague.

Since I'd already allotted time to stop at the law office, I decided to swing by there anyway.

And was really glad I did when I bumped into a friend of Mary's, Fred Durham, in the outer lobby. We exchanged pleasantries, and I asked if he had a few minutes.

"Sure. Come up to my office."

Fred was the law firm's tech geek. He was on the premises during the day and on call 24/7— in case a computer glitch threatened to make a motion late or cause one of the attorneys to have to go to court without vital papers or information.

He also helped the paralegals, like Mary, with online research. Both shy introverts, he and Mary had become friends. He might be an even better person to talk to than Larry Bevans.

Fred's office was minuscule. I'd seen bigger broom closets. Or maybe it seemed small because it was crammed with computer equipment.

He shoved papers and books off his only visitor's chair, made a have-a-seat gesture, then settled his own bulk into his desk chair. Small tables on either side of him held various sized metal boxes with colored lights blinking. One had several appendages sticking up and I thought it might be a router. The others, I was clueless.

At least his small office had a window, which made it somewhat less claustrophobic. A short bookcase sat under it, and more papers and books were jammed on the bottom shelves. But across the top were neatly arranged, labeled bins, with metal and plastic objects—no doubt, computer parts—in them.

We made small talk, awkwardly, while I tried to decide how to broach the subject. Mary might not appreciate me telling her coworkers that she was assaulted.

I leaned forward. "Fred, can you think of anyone who might be stalking Mary? She's had some strange things happen lately."

His broad face sagged. "What kind of things?"

I shrugged. Ad-libbing, I said, "Weird emails. Feeling like she's being followed. And some of the emails, they had things in them that nobody would know except really close friends."

He ran a hand over dark hair. Its ends dangled unevenly slightly above his collar. He was in serious need of a haircut. "Is that why she's out today?"

"Yes," I said, "she's pretty spooked."

"I can't think of anybody around here who pays extra attention to her." His chair creaked as he adjusted his weight. "If she's talked about things in emails to her close friends, those are pretty easy to hack into."

I made a mental note to check her laptop to see what she might have shared through her personal email account.

"Can you get me into her office email, by any chance?" I fully expected Fred to say no, maybe even be horrified that I'd asked.

Without answering me, he tapped on his keyboard, then swung his monitor around so we both could see it. "I can remote access any computer in the firm, since I sometimes have to troubleshoot things quickly. Here's her email account but I don't know the password."

I thought for a moment. Mary was almost as computer savvy as Fred was. She'd told me one time that passwords should be coded messages about something important to you, so you could remember them. But they should not include info that others would have access to. She'd said her laptop's password contained her oldest nephew's due date, which even his own mother, her sister, had long since forgotten. But Mary had been so excited about becoming an auntie that the date was seared into her brain.

"May I?" I pointed to the keyboard. Fred shoved it over in front of me.

I typed in my initials and birthday and got an error message.

"You only get three tries," Fred said.

I tried Annaleise's initials and her birth date. I got another error message.

I was about to ask Fred his birthday when a morbid thought crossed my mind.

"What happens if I use up the three chances?" I asked him.

He gave me a small grin. "I can reset it, but I don't like to do that. It could lead back to me."

"And these attempts won't?"

"Nope, I'm using a VPN."

Thanks to Phillip, I actually knew what that was. "Okay," I said, "I have one more idea."

Sometimes Annaleise had ended emails from both her and Charles with an abbreviated signature, *Ann&Char*. I typed that in, followed by the date of their death.

The email account opened and a list of messages appeared on the screen.

"All right!" Fred dragged the keyboard back in front of himself but left the monitor slanted so we both could see it. "What are we looking for? Give me some keywords."

"Hmm, *Nick* and *fat*."

Fred typed them in and a list of several emails popped up, all dated the same day, and all sent from a soulmates-dot-com address.

"Mary was using a dating service?" Fred said, sounding a little hurt.

"Yeah, I was surprised too when I found out."

He shot me a look that I couldn't readily interpret, then clicked on the first few messages, in quick succession. Too quick for me to read them.

"It looks like when she answered this X guy, it went through their server, but when she's notified that he's sent her a message, the message shows up in her email." Fred turned the monitor slightly farther toward me.

He'd somehow stacked multiple windows on the screen, each with an open email in it. They read like one side of a conversation. And that conversation was obviously about Mary's ex calling her fat.

"Okay, try *Navy doll* in the search engine," I said.

Only one message popped up. Fred opened it.

Wait, do I have this right? You have a doll dressed in a Navy uniform from WWI?

I sighed and repeated a few choice curse words inside my head. I'd hope we'd be able to narrow down suspects, maybe find someone Mary worked with who might have hacked into her soulmates account. Instead, anyone who managed to get into her work email account could have gotten the information that Mary thought only X knew.

But only if they knew Mary's password. She was too smart to leave it lying around, and I doubted she needed to write it down anyway. Indeed, she probably used it as her password to make sure she never forgot her friends.

I swallowed a small lump and said, "Search for X and the word *cologne*."

Fred tapped on the keyboard, then shook his head.

How about *fragrance*?"

Fred tapped away, and his face brightened. Again, he opened several windows, revealing one side of a conversation about favorite fragrances. In one of them, X had written *I love the scent of roses.*

"Roses," Fred said. "That's Mary's favorite perfume."

"Yes." I pointed to another of X's messages. *My aftershave is kind of woodsy, I guess.* He mentioned a brand I didn't recognize. I grabbed a small pack of blank post-its from the pile of papers now on the floor. "May I?"

"Sure." Fred handed me a pen, and I wrote down the name of the aftershave.

"Now, search for *X* and my name, *James.*"

His thick fingers danced on the keys. "There's only one email."

He clicked on it. *Sounds like you and James are really good friends. Should I be jealous?* came up on the monitor.

Fred pulled it back around, so I couldn't see the screen anymore, and typed something else. He frowned.

"What?"

Another quick sideways glance. "She doesn't mention me to him at all." Then Fred's cheeks turned pink.

What does that mean? Did Fred see us as competitors for Mary's friendship?

I opened my mouth, wanting to reassure him. It's not like Mary's affection for her friends had limits or anything. But I hesitated. I might be misreading his body language, and wouldn't that be embarrassing?

"Is there any way to check if others have hacked into her email?"

"Yeah," Fred said, "but that might take awhile."

I glanced at my phone. I only had a half hour to get across town for my audition. "I gotta run. Can you call me if you find out anything?" I jotted my cell number on another post-it and handed it to him.

Fred grinned. "Not *if*, when. *When* I find out something."

I smiled back, stood, and offered him my hand. "Thanks, man."

His palm was a bit clammy as he shook my hand. "Let me know if you think of anything else I can help with," he said. "And tell Mary I miss her. Hope she comes back to work soon."

"I will."

I was hustling out the front door of the law firm's offices when I spotted Larry Bevans getting off the elevator. I waved.

"Hey, James," he said as he approached, juggling his briefcase and offering his hand. "Sorry I can't talk right now. On my way to a client meeting. But are you going to be in town this evening? Wanna meet for dinner?"

I hadn't planned to stay over, but I really did want to pick this guy's brain. "Sure. Where do you want to meet?"

He named a restaurant. "Say, six-thirty?"

"Sounds good." I sketched him a quick salute and headed for the fire stairs. No time to wait for the elevator and I was only on the third floor.

Mary

I'd been reading most of the day on James's sofa, trying to immerse myself in fictional worlds. Halfway through the second novel, I drifted off into blessed oblivion.

Awhile later, a sound woke me. I listened intently but heard only silence.

Then the faint tinkling of wind chimes. I assumed it came from the back patio, on the other side of the French doors to my left. I tried to go back to sleep.

The tinkling sound again, louder.

And again, even louder and faster, somehow sounding urgent.

I jerked upright on the sofa, my heart rate kicking up a couple of notches. I stared at the French doors, but I couldn't see much. The afternoon sun was on the other side of the house, casting long shadows over the patio.

I was thinking I would go out and find those damn wind chimes, and take them down so they'd stop interrupting my nap, when the doors burst open.

I froze, my brain refusing to process what was happening.

A man, all in black, including a ski mask, stood in the doorway.

I jumped up. But he was on me before I could run. We fell back onto the sofa.

Heart pounding, I fought like a demon. *This can't be. Not again!* I scratched, clawed, and bucked under him, no air available to make a sound.

A woodsy scent, combined with that of male sweat, made my stomach roil.

A floor lamp near the sofa came crashing down, the heavy wrought-iron pole slamming into the man's head.

He collapsed on top of me. I grabbed the front of his black windbreaker and shoved him aside. Scrambling out from under him, I almost tripped over the fallen lamp.

He moaned, and I bolted for the front door.

I ran across the lawn to Carrie's house. It wasn't until I was on her porch that I was able to catch my breath enough to scream.

CHAPTER SEVEN

James

I was really, really glad I'd made it to the audition. Because I got the part—leading man! Those roles would be getting harder to land now that I was in my forties.

The afternoon had been spent signing the contract and doing other paperwork, then meetings with the producer and my leading lady.

Around five-forty, I texted Mary with the good news, hoping it would cheer her up some. The play was by a playwright she loved, and I knew she'd be front and center on opening night.

But I got no response. Maybe she was napping. I texted Carrie next. Also no response.

Worry niggled at my stomach. I shook it off.

Carrie didn't keep her phone on her person when she was home, at least not anymore. Not since her abusive ex-husband met his demise. No longer carrying it everywhere around the house was a sign of her liberation, she had said.

She kept it by her purse, so she wouldn't forget it when she left the house. Maybe she was out back gardening, or sitting on the front porch enjoying the sunny afternoon. Thanks to a cold front that had blown through the area last night, the temperature hovered around seventy-nine, with low humidity—a short reprieve from the summer heat.

Indeed, the early evening was so nice, I decided to walk to the restaurant where I was meeting Larry Bevans. I had plenty of time.

Halfway there, I spotted a Sephora's store.

This is my lucky day!

I went in. A helpful saleslady said she would be happy to show me to the display of men's fragrances.

Of course she would be—X's brand of aftershave cost a small fortune.

Carrie

A scream!

I whirled around from the utility sink in the mud room, where I'd been cleaning paintbrushes.

It had come from out front. I bolted through the kitchen and to the front door, threw it open. Mary stood, sobbing, on the porch.

"What happened?"

Her shoulders shook with raking sobs, but she pointed to James's house. "Him!" she finally managed to get out.

I dragged her inside, sat her on my sofa. "Phillip!" I yelled as I headed to the kitchen.

The gun safe came off the top shelf of a cabinet, its key retrieved from a drawer. The box of cartridges was in a different cabinet. I'd finished loading the gun when Phillip appeared in the doorway.

"Wha's up?"

"I think someone's broken into James's house. Call 911, keep the doors locked and stick close to Mary."

I pushed past him and stopped by the sofa.

Mary was still sobbing softly. She looked up at me, swallowed hard. "He came in the back, through the French doors. I went out the front."

Phillip entered the room. I nodded at him and dashed out our front door. It slammed behind me, the deadbolt snicking closed.

My chest swelled with pride—damn, I had a good kid, no questions asked, just take action. But at the same time, my heart was heavy. A fifteen-year-old should not be so savvy about how to ward off attackers.

The sun brushed the tops of the tree line up by the road, casting long shadows on the driveway and spot-lighting the front of James's house.

The front door was closed. I doubted Mary took the time to close it behind her.

I raced across the strip of lawn between the houses and came to a halt at the bottom of the porch steps. Sticking close to the side of the house, I eased my way around back, peeking in windows as I went. No one in the kitchen. The living room drapes were pulled closed.

The French doors were also closed.

What was going on? It crossed my mind that Mary might have been napping and she'd dreamed the whole thing. She and I would both feel like fools if the sheriff's department showed up and there was no sign of an intruder.

I took a step closer to the doors, reached for a knob. And smelled it...the faint odor of gasoline. I froze, squinted through the glass in the door.

A line of red flames galloped across the living room rug, toward the sofa.

I jumped back, barely in time. The sofa went up with a loud whoosh.

And the French doors blew open.

———◆———

James

I'd gotten us a table at the restaurant when my phone pinged. It was Bevans, texting to say he'd gotten tied up and couldn't make dinner after all. *Rain check?*

Sure, I replied, then thought, *Well, damn!* There was no point in staying in the city now. I could be home before full dark if I left right away. I'd grab a fast-food dinner along the way to Virginia.

I retrieved my car from the parking garage, paid the exorbitant daily fee, and headed out of DC. It was the tail end of rush hour, so the streets were still semi-clogged. I had finally shaken loose from the city traffic and was on country roads—forty minutes from home—when my phone rang.

"James, get home as quick as you can." Carrie's voice was breathless. "Someone's attacked Mary and set your house on fire."

CHAPTER EIGHT

Mary

Phillip stood by the front window. Suddenly he gasped. "Oh my God, James's house, it's on fire!"

He bolted to the front door, flung it open and was gone. Ginger raced after him.

I jumped up from the sofa and closed and locked the door, then ran to the window. Smoke billowed above the roof next door.

I fumbled my phone from my pocket and called 911. A moment of confusion when I couldn't remember the street number. I'd been coming to James's house for so many years, I knew the way by heart and had long since forgotten the actual address.

A strange clanking sound wasn't helping. I couldn't get my mind to focus.

"James Fitzgerald's place," I yelled into the phone. "A boy just called to have the sheriff sent out here."

"Yes, okay," the dispatcher said. "I've got it. Sheriff should be there soon. I'm sending the fire department as well."

I stared out the window for minutes that felt like hours, praying that Carrie and Phillip were safe. But I was too chicken to leave the house to look for them.

Smoke roiled around James's house, blurring my view of it.

Please, please, get here! I silently urged the fire engine.

The clanking sound again, louder.

What the hell is that?

A face popped up in the picture window, black ski mask, big grin.

I screamed and dropped my phone, then froze for a second.

The man raised his hand. He held a brick.

Heart pounding, I bolted for the back of the house, the sound of glass shattering behind me.

Out the kitchen door. I stumbled on the back porch steps, grabbed for the railing. It was sticky with fresh paint.

I ran to the tall wooden gate in the back fence. Carrie usually locked it at night, but now the padlock hung open on the latch. I grabbed the lock, flung the gate open, then slammed it shut behind me. I managed to get my hand through the gap between fence post and gate and maneuver the lock back through the hole in the latch. I locked it.

That oughta slow the bastard down!

I turned and stopped in my tracks. Several cars and pickup trucks were now parked in the two driveways and yards. People were getting out of them and hauling firefighting gear—boots, yellow jackets and helmets—from the beds and trunks of their vehicles.

Volunteer firefighters! In the country, they often went directly to the fire location rather than the station.

A siren screamed from the road behind the trees. Glimpses of flashing red lights. Then a fire engine was bouncing down the lane.

I started to run to the nearest man, but stopped short again. He stood next to a vehicle, wearing a black t-shirt and jeans.

He could be a fireman, or my attacker! Any of these men could be the bastard. All he had to do was pull off his mask and the long-sleeved windbreaker and...

I frantically looked around. There were two sheriff's department cruisers in James's driveway but I didn't see Wallace or his deputies.

I turned toward James's house. Smoke whirled around it. Flames crackled, then hissed as fire hoses were aimed at them.

I couldn't hide in a burning building, and who knew where Carrie and Phillip were? I screamed, in frustration this time. The sound was drowned out by a crash as something collapsed inside the house.

I whirled around and ran for the woods.

James

I broke every speed limit getting home, and made it just as dusk was settling over the countryside.

A few hundred feet from my driveway, half a car was suddenly in my path. I swerved into the other lane—thank God, no one was coming—and missed side-swiping the dark sedan by a coat of paint.

I stomped on the brakes—a bad idea. My car went into a stomach-clenching spin, stopping back in my rightful lane but headed the wrong way. My headlights lit up the car I'd almost hit. It was parked on the narrow shoulder. Woods looming close beside the country road had forced the driver, who didn't seem to be present, to leave it sticking out part-way onto the asphalt.

I took a deep breath, got my car turned around again and raced down my driveway. A fire engine blocked my way. I got out and ran.

All of my front yard and half of Carrie's were full of emergency vehicles, plus the cars of the volunteer firefighters, who would've raced to the scene from various parts of the county. Headlights and spotlights made it brighter than high noon.

And my brick house stood in the middle of it all, looking totally normal, except for wisps of smoke curling above its roof.

Carrie bolted out of the shadows and threw herself at me. I barely managed to stay on my feet.

Half sobbing, she said, "Mary's gone."

"What!?"

"She's gone," she repeated. "I left her and Phillip in my house while I went to investigate–"

I opened my mouth.

"With my gun," she quickly added.

I shut my mouth again. Carrie knew her way around guns and was no shrinking violet when it came to protecting those she cared about. But still I hated that she'd put herself at risk like that.

"I was in the back when the fire started," she was saying. "It was obviously set. Phillip had already called 911, because the guy attacked Mary."

"He attacked her again?" I said.

Carrie nodded. "She fought him off this time. Phillip said he was watching out the front window and saw smoke coming from your house, so he ran over to find me. A few seconds later, he heard Mary scream, and she came out the back gate, ran toward your house, then turned and took off for the woods. He thought he saw a man running after her. But the air was smoky, and he wasn't sure."

"The house looks okay," I said, rather inanely. My mind was reeling, trying to process all this.

"Not so much in the back. They've got the fire mostly out now. It started in the living room."

"Oh." My heart sank. But I forced my mind to focus on the more important issue—finding Mary.

Mary

Common sense was asserting itself over panic, and I was realizing that taking off into the woods hadn't been a great idea. But it had seemed like the only option.

I could hear someone crashing through the trees behind me.

"Mary, wait!" A man's voice.

I tried to suck in more air, to ease the stitch in my side. I made myself keep running.

The crashing sounds were getting closer. "Mary, stop. It's me, X. I mean Avi. I'm not going to hurt you."

Yeah, right. I saw a dark area ahead, realized it was a group of trees close together. I ducked behind the biggest one and clamped a hand over my mouth, forcing myself to breathe through my nose.

The rasping sound that made was only slightly quieter than my panting had been. I willed my heart and lungs to slow down. Neither organ listened.

A dark shadow ran by on the path. *Avi!*

I held my breath, stayed frozen for what felt like several minutes. Then I dropped my hand from my mouth and drew in a long shuddering breath.

I stepped carefully back onto the path, looking around. But the sky was darkening into night and the shadows were so deep I could hardly make out anything.

I turned back the way I'd come.

A form jumped out of the darkness and grabbed me in a bear hug.

I screamed and stomped on his nearest foot. It stood out in a white sneaker against the dark path.

He yelped, loosened his grip. I struggled free.

"Mary, please give me a chance to explain. I came out here to make sure you're okay. I'm not gonna hurt you."

Confusion invaded my brain, but my pounding heart was demanding I get the hell out of there. I took off, back toward the houses and the bright lights flashing at the edge of the woods.

I bolted from the line of trees, then stopped, my sides heaving. The sheriff and two deputies were running toward me.

"Are you okay, Ms. Hanson?" the sheriff yelled.

"Yes, but my attacker's in the woods, right behind me," I called back.

The deputies went into the trees and the sheriff stopped beside me. "You sure you're all right?"

I nodded mutely. *Physically*, I thought. Mentally was a different story. I was pretty sure I would never stop shaking.

The deputies came out of the woods, with X/Avi between them. He was struggling some to break free, but they had a good hold on his arms. They stopped about fifteen feet away. He tried to pull toward me. The deputies dug in their heels.

"Mary, I didn't mean to frighten you," he called out, his face contorted. "I came to make sure you were okay, and when I saw the house on fire and you running toward the woods..."

My stomach churned. I trembled with fear. But for whom? For myself, or for him?

He terrified me, but at the same time, my chest ached. I wanted to yell at the deputies, "Don't hurt him."

Was this how battered women felt, this conflict between loving the man and fearing him at the same time?

Nick had been abusive verbally and emotionally, but he'd never hit me. I was afraid of his scorn but never for my physical safety.

My confusion kept me rooted to the ground.

X/Avi pulled one arm loose. His eyes were shiny.

Is he trying not to cry?

He took a couple steps, dragging the other guy with him. "Please forgive me, Mary. I didn't mean to make things worse."

The first deputy jumped forward and grabbed his shoulder.

The sheriff waved a hand at the deputies. I startled. I'd forgotten he was there beside me.

"Get him out of here," he ordered.

Then he gently took my elbow and steered me toward the emergency vehicles cluttering the yards.

I did finally stop shaking...after I'd been hugged nearly to death by James and Carrie. Even Phillip mumbled, "Glad you're okay." He was hanging onto Ginger's collar. Carrie told him to take the dog back to their house.

Then a paramedic led me to an ambulance and sat me down on the back bumper. He laid a light blanket around my shoulders and gave me a wet cloth to wipe the paint from my hand, while he checked me over.

The inane thought crossed my mind that I owed Carrie an apology for messing up her fresh paint on the railing.

The sheriff came over. The paramedic gave him a nod.

"You feel up to comin' around back," the sheriff said, "and tellin' us what happened?"

"I guess," I said. Standing, I tried to return the blanket to the paramedic.

"Keep it," he said, his eyes kind.

I almost burst into tears at that small gesture.

I followed the sheriff around to the back of James's house, and gasped. A gaping black hole was where the French doors used to be.

The sheriff stopped at the threshold. "The fire captain ain't sure it's safe for us to go in, but can you point out what happened where?"

James came up on the other side of me. He wrapped an arm around my shoulders and squeezed, then let go. Carrie stood slightly behind us. She patted my back twice, through the blanket. I tried not to cringe at the contact from either of them, even though I was grateful for their support.

Floodlights had been set up outside the hole, shining into the burnt-out room.

I pointed at the lump that had been the sofa. A charred beam lay across it.

I took a deep breath. "I was napping when I heard a noise. I thought at first I'd imagine it or maybe dreamed it. But I heard it again. I was about to get up and investigate when the doors crashed open and a man stood there. He was all in black, had a ski mask on. The same height and build as before. The same guy. And he...he was on top of me...before I could do anything."

The sheriff nodded encouragement. "Take your time. You're doin' fine."

"We were struggling, and the sofa must've moved and shoved into the floor lamp at the end of it. It crashed down on his head, and I got loose and ran to Carrie's house."

James took a step forward and turned slightly to look in my face. "Are you sure the sofa moved?" he asked.

"Um, it must have."

His expression was skeptical.

What...didn't he believe me?

"I mean, I didn't feel the couch move, but I wasn't paying attention to that. I was fighting for my life."

"I know, I know." James's expression softened. He reached out to touch my arm.

I pulled back some, hugged the blanket closer, indignation tightening my chest. "I certainly didn't imagine the lamp coming down on his head!"

"No, no, of course not," James and the sheriff said in unison.

Carrie nudged James aside a little and put her arm around my shoulders. "Can I take her back to my house now?" she asked the sheriff.

He nodded. "We're holdin' this Xavier fella for now, in 'protective custody,'" he made air quotes, "until I can talk to his handler and figure out what the devil is goin' on."

My stomach felt queasy. I wasn't sure what to think about X/Avi at this point. I didn't want him to be my attacker, but what were the odds that he *and* the attacker would show up at the same time?

Carrie had started to turn us away when the sheriff said, "Oh, one other thing. That noise you heard, that woke you up. What was it?"

I glanced around. There was nothing on James's back patio that could have made that sound. I shook my head. "I know it doesn't make sense, but I could've sworn I heard wind chimes, tinkling in the breeze."

Carrie twisted around and exchanged an intense look with James.

What the H does that mean?

CHAPTER NINE

Carrie

I steered Mary toward my house, longing for a hot shower. My stomach grumbled. And dinner. We'd need to do something about food soon.

Mary stopped in front of me and I almost plowed into her.

I glanced past her. Phillip stood on the front porch, his face worried. Ginger sat beside him.

"Mom..." he said hesitantly.

Then I saw it. The hole where a picture window should've been.

"Ginger's not reacting," Phillip said, "so I don't think anybody's in there, but I thought I should wait."

"You did the right thing," I said, pulling out the pistol that, somewhere along the way, I'd stuffed in the back of my shorts' waistband.

Mary's hand covered her mouth. "Oh, no. I forgot to tell the sheriff about the window. The guy in the ski mask put a brick through it. That's why I ran out the back."

"We'll call him in a bit. But first..." I trailed off, debating. Leave Phillip and her out here on the porch or take them with me? Leaving them hadn't worked out so well last time.

I gestured with my left hand, the right one holding the pistol up in front of me. "Stick close behind me."

The three of us searched the house. As Phillip had predicted, no one was there. We locked the doors and then stood in the living room, staring at the hole.

I've got some wood scraps in the basement," I said. "There's probably one big enough to cover that. But I'll need some help getting it upstairs."

"The problem is," Phillip said, "if we all go down there to get the wood, someone can come through that hole while we're gone."

I tried to hand my pistol to Mary.

She shook her head. "You're the one who knows how to use it. You should stay here. Phillip and I can get the wood."

"It's heavy."

She gave me an exasperated look. "I'm not fragile. I can help carry a piece of wood up some steps."

My chest tightened. I wasn't sure why. I nodded. "You're right. It's in the back, left corner."

Phillip headed for the door to the basement, Mary right behind him.

"And bring up some nails and the hammer," I called after them.

James

I'd been dreading this moment for months, ever since Annaleise's death. The moment when I would have to tell one of my friends—one of *her* friends—that my house was haunted by her ghost.

Well maybe *haunted* wasn't the right word. She was a friendly ghost, protective of me and Carrie, and now of

Mary as well. That wasn't surprising since she and Mary had been close, especially after Mary's divorce.

How would Mary take the news about her friend being a ghost now? She'd had more than enough shocks for one day. Maybe I should wait until tomorrow.

I had gotten a short reprieve, while finishing up with the sheriff's people and the fire department. Then I called the clean-up company that the fire captain had recommended.

Out of excuses to procrastinate, I took a deep breath and went over to Carrie's house.

I froze—one foot in the air, about to step up on the porch—and stared at plywood where glass should be.

I went to the door and knocked. "It's me, James." I could've used my key but didn't particularly want Carrie to shoot me if I took her by surprise.

She pulled open the door, and I tilted my head toward the boarded-up window.

"That's why Mary went out the back," she said. "Mr. Ski Mask bashed it in after Phillip ran to find me."

"Where's Mary?" I asked.

"Lying down in the spare room upstairs."

The old farmhouse had four bedrooms upstairs, plus the paneled study on the ground floor that Phillip had taken over as his "man cave." The room Carrie referred to was the only one that was furnished, other than the master—and then only sparsely with a day bed and small nightstand.

"Let's go into the kitchen," Carrie said in a low voice. "We need to talk."

She had already made tea, black for me and chamomile for herself. She knew I hated chamomile.

"I'm wondering if we're doing the right thing," she said, as we both sat down at her small table.

"What do you mean?"

"Is it really helpful for Mary to be here now, isolated like this out in the boonies?"

A slight tightening in my chest. "Well, I had to bring her here. Her apartment door was busted open." I heard the defensive note in my voice.

Sometimes the hyper-awareness of tone and body language—that's part of being a good actor—spills over into real life, which can be annoying...and distracting.

I tuned back into what Carrie was saying in mid-sentence. "...*ask* her if that's what she wanted to do?"

"No, yes." I thought back. I probably hadn't asked, just announced, *I'm taking you to Virginia.* "She was in no shape at the time to make a decision."

Carrie's expression said she was trying hard to be patient. "Is the door secured now?"

My chest tightened again. "Yeah, the locksmith emailed me the bill, and I paid it already."

Carrie pursed her lips. "You *paid* Mary's locksmith bill?"

"Yes, because *I* can afford it better than she can," I snapped.

"Did you ask her if that was okay?"

"No."

Carrie was staring at me now.

"What?" I said. More pressure was building in my chest, and a lump had formed in my throat. My cheeks heated. It was an old feeling, one I hadn't felt in years. "Are you *scolding* me?"

Carrie's face softened. "No, of course not."

The tension in my chest continued. What the hell was going on here?

"It's just that," she averted her eyes, "you can be overprotective at times."

"And you think that's what's happening now," I said in an angry voice.

"No...maybe. I'm only wondering what's best for Mary."

I let silence spin out as I tried to ease the tightness with a deep breath. It didn't work.

"I mean," Carrie continued, "You brought her out here to keep her safe, which made sense then. But now...apparently, we can't keep her safe unless one of us is always with her–"

"So," I said through gritted teeth, "one of us will always be with her."

"We can't do that forever." She paused. "Why are you so angry?"

"I'm not angry," I snapped again. But my tone definitely belied the words. "I just don't like being criticized about how I deal with my friends."

Carrie pressed her lips together, then took a deep breath. "What's going on, James? You usually accept feedback better than this."

I let out a short bark of humorless laughter. "Oh, not much going on, only someone tried to burn down my house, after attacking a good friend. Again!"

She sighed. "Which brings me to another point. Maybe *we're* not safe out here in the boonies with Mary here as well."

I opened my mouth, but she held up a hand. "My main concern though," she said, "is that we've taken over control of Mary's life. And I'm not sure that's good for her emotionally."

I struggled to rein in my anger and think straight. "What are you suggesting?"

"That we *ask* her what she wants to do. And maybe brainstorm with her about how to keep her safe, until the DNA results come back on this Avi guy."

That sounded quite rational, but still I fought with the tension in my body and the crazy thoughts racing through my head. It did *feel* like Carrie was scolding me, that she was disappointed in me. And I realized that under the anger was guilt.

Now I was totally confused. Had I done the wrong thing for Mary? Had my efforts to protect her made her more vulnerable? Out here in the boonies, as Carrie put it.

I shook my head but managed to get out, "Okay, we'll ask her."

"And we need to tell her about Annaleise," Carrie said.

I shook my head harder. "I'm not sure she's up for that shock right now."

Carrie frowned. "I think she's stronger than you give her credit for."

Anger surged again. I bit my lower lip to keep from saying something I'd regret.

"Look, James, I don't want to argue."

"*That* feeling is mutual," I said, my tone acerbic.

Carrie fell silent, watching me. She picked up her now cold tea and took a sip.

"Mary's a gentle soul," I said, striving for a more reasonable tone of voice.

"Agreed, but that doesn't mean she's weak. She's already survived a lot."

I nodded slightly, begrudgingly admitting that point. "Okay, we'll talk to her about the safety issue first, and see how that goes. Then *I'll* decide if she's up to hearing about Annaleise. She is *my* friend."

Carrie let out a soft sigh. "She's become my friend, too," she said with exaggerated patience. "But I'll concede that you know her better. If you don't bring up Annaleise, I'll follow your lead. Then we can talk privately again about when to go there."

"Or if we should *ever* go there."

Carrie tilted her head to one side. "Why wouldn't we tell her eventually?"

I sat still for a beat, trying to sort out the lump of dread in my gut that I got every time I thought about telling Mary that one of her closest friends was now a ghost. "Knowing about Annaleise is a mixed bag," I finally said. "At first it was really comforting to feel her presence, once I got over the shock..." I trailed off.

"But?" Carrie said after a moment.

"Well, it still feels good to have her around, but it also makes me feel selfish and guilty. She's trapped in this place. What is that like for her? Not being able to go anywhere but these two properties. And lately..." I sighed. "It almost feels sad rather than reassuring when I hear the wind chimes."

"It's keeping the grief stirred up?" Carrie asked in a soft voice.

"Maybe."

After a long stretch of silence, she said, "So you want to protect Mary from those conflicting feelings?"

"Yes. What's wrong with that?" I demanded.

Now Carrie sat quietly for a moment, her expression thoughtful.

"I think the line between protecting and controlling is a thin one," she eventually said. "And the line between controlling and abusive is also a fine one."

Several emotions did battle inside of me. Anger flared in my chest. Had she just said I was abusive? But a calmer part of my brain was saying, *Take it easy. You're over-reacting*.

When she didn't elaborate, I said, "So that's why you get kinda..." I paused, sensing I should pick my words carefully. "Um, a little defensive sometimes, when I try to protect you? You're afraid I'll slide toward abusive, like your ex."

She nodded. "And you usually back off, which I appreciate."

"Because I've learned that you can take care of yourself."

She snorted softly. "I guess facing down a couple of killers together would do that."

I chuckled, even though there was nothing humorous about the memories. But those experiences had forged the bond between us. And a deeper trust than most couples achieve in years.

Finally, the tension in my body eased completely. This was Carrie I was talking to, the least judgmental person I'd ever met. I almost laughed at myself.

Carrie looked up, past my shoulder, and her eyes went wide. I whirled around in my seat.

Mary stood in the kitchen doorway.

How long had she been there?

Carrie

I wasn't surprised that Mary had already given the situation a great deal of thought.

"I need to go back to DC, and back to work, otherwise the bastard..." She trailed off.

"...has won," I said softly.

She bit her lip and nodded.

"Are you sure you're going to be okay," James said, "in the apartment by yourself?"

"The lock's fixed, right?"

"Yes," he said, "and the doorframe is now reinforced with metal."

Mary and I both stared across the kitchen table at James.

Heat was building in my chest. Why would he do that without consulting Mary first?

"How much was all that?" she asked, a slight tremor in her voice.

I had a cousin who was a paralegal. I knew they made decent money, but living in DC was expensive.

James shrugged. "Not bad. Two-hundred, forty and change."

I suspected that figure was maybe one third of the full amount of the bill.

Mary shook her head. "I'll Venmo you two-fifty each month for the next three months."

I snorted. "You know him well."

Mary actually flashed a quick grin.

James glanced at me and then at the wall above the kitchen window.

I followed his line of vision, but it took a moment for my eyes to focus on the wall clock there. No wonder my vision was blurry—it was almost midnight.

I met his gaze and gave a small nod. We'd wait until tomorrow to tell her about–

"So, what's the deal with the wind chimes?" Mary asked.

James and I exchanged another look, and we both sighed.

"Do you remember what Annaleise's laughter sounded like?" James said.

"Yeah, it was kind of a tinkling sound." Her face lit up. "That's the wind chimes! She's..." She stuttered to a stop and paled. "She's a ghost?"

James nodded. "The wind chime sound is the main way she communicates. She can even somehow make them sound angry or sad, and she warns us with the sound, like–"

"Like she warned me this afternoon." Mary sat up straighter in her chair. "And that was the clanking sound I heard just before the bastard showed up here and broke the window."

James nodded again. "Yes, it can sound like that when it's a warning." He paused. "And she can move things, but I've only seen her do that when she's really mad and trying to protect us." He tilted his head toward me.

Mary's eyes went wide.

"I've seen her throw books mainly," James added. "And a small statue once. But that floor lamp, it's normally several feet away. I doubt the sofa moved and hit it."

Her eyes went even wider. "That lamp is wrought iron. She could lift that?"

James shrugged. "She knocked a bookcase over once. It was full of books."

"Poor Annaleise." Tears pooled in Mary's eyes. "She's stuck here. We have to help her."

CHAPTER TEN

Carrie

I glanced at James. He looked as taken aback as I was.

I wasn't sure why we were so surprised, though. James's house had once had two ghosts—Annaleise and his mother. But once Annaleise's killer had been found, and my abusive husband was taken out of the picture, we had thought we were safe and could live in peace.

James's mother had made fewer and fewer appearances after that. Until one day, we'd realized that she had let go and moved on.

And now poor Annaleise didn't even have her company, in whatever place she resided. If it was a place at all. Maybe her spirit just drifted in the air.

"Yes, we should help her to move on," I said. "But not until after your attacker has been caught. She's far better than a burglar alarm. And that should be a factor in staying overnight in DC. Here, you have Annaleise to warn you."

I sighed. Maybe I shouldn't be encouraging her to stay here. I didn't like the idea of Phillip being in jeopardy. But she was important to James—very important—and I cared about her too.

Besides, I reminded myself, *it's not my decision. Mary's life, Mary's decision.*

"True," she was saying. "Maybe we can find out how long the DNA results will take." She paused. "I don't know if I want it to be Avi, so he can be prosecuted and I can get on with my life. Or that it's not him, so we can still...you know..."

"Get to know each other better," I offered.

She nodded. "Anyway, maybe I should stay here at night at least, until those results come in. I mean, if you don't mind, Carrie?"

"No, I don't mind. There's plenty of room here."

I turned to James. "Do we need to do anything to secure your house tonight?"

He shook his head. "It can't be made all that secure, but the firemen tacked a tarp over the hole in the back wall. That will keep the elements and the critters out, at least."

"Then let's go to bed, and decide tomorrow when you're going back to DC, Mary." I quickly added, "Unless you want to go back to work tomorrow?"

She bit her lip again. "I think I'll wait one more day. See what we can find out tomorrow."

"Sounds like a plan." James pushed himself to a stand.

Mary and I started up the stairs. I assumed James was right behind me, but I heard rustling in the kitchen. I looked over my shoulder.

James was pulling the box of ammo out of the cabinet.

I saw Mary to her room and acted like I was going into the master. But once her door was shut, I went back downstairs.

James was spreading a sheet over the leather sofa in the living room. My pistol rested on the pillow that he'd also pulled out of the linen closet.

He looked up at me. "I'd much rather be in your bed," he said in a low voice.

"You've had a long day," I said. "I'll stay down here. You go to bed."

He shook his head.

"We've got the alarm system and Ginger." I was trying to decide if I should be pissed. I wasn't sure I had the energy for a full-blown argument.

"I doubt I'd be able to sleep up there," he said. "I'd be jumping at every noise this old house makes, worrying about what was going on down here."

My mind veered to my earlier thoughts. *We'd thought that we were safe, could live in peace.* My stomach turned queasy.

For a moment, resentment bubbled in my chest. I tamped it down. *Do we really have a choice here?* Mary was like family to James.

He strode across the room and tenderly cupped my face with his hands. Then, he gave me a long, sweet kiss.

Heat spread through me, followed by a tingling sensation. I told myself to settle down.

When he let go of me, I gave him a small nod and went back upstairs.

I tossed and turned, telling myself I was anxious about the situation we were in, the risks to our safety. And I was.

But the *whole* truth was that my body ached for James. I wanted him lying beside me. Better still if he were holding me, making love to me.

This is ridiculous, I thought, as tears leaked from the corners of my eyes.

I'd never felt this way about Greg. I'd thought that I'd loved him, but it had been some kind of sick need—not love at all. More a longing for something I'd never had, not since my father had died when I was fifteen.

And, I admitted to myself in the darkness of my bedroom, even before that. My father had been loving, but in a distant, preoccupied way. It was like he'd partially walled himself off from his bitter wife, his gay son, and his needy daughter.

I angrily punched my pillow and willed myself to go to sleep.

But that probably wasn't going to happen until I gave in to the tears stinging the back of my eyes.

James

Carrie is an early riser. As soon as she came downstairs, I told her my plans for the morning.

She nodded and yawned. "Be careful."

"I'm sure they have Avi in a cell."

She gave me a small smile. "I *meant* don't piss off the sheriff."

I chuckled and headed out the door.

Carrie caught up with me and threw her arms around my neck. She kissed me, hard. "I missed you last night," she whispered.

I held her tight for a moment, warmth swelling in my chest. "I missed you too."

Then I tore myself away.

I found Avi lounging in a visitor's chair in front of the sheriff's desk.

Wallace's shaggy eyebrows went up at my surprised look. He answered the unasked question. "Xavier here reminded me this mornin' that I have no evidence he's actually committed any crime. So I let him outta his cell, as long as he agreed to keep me company 'til his handler gets here."

"Do you mind if he and I have a little chat?" I asked.

"Not at all," the sheriff said. "I got some paperwork to do."

"Let's go outside, Avi. Or do you prefer X now?"

He shook his head. "I go by my middle name, Paul, most of the time now," he said, as we exited the building. "But I like it when you call me Avi." He smiled. "Brings back fond memories."

I gave him a fake smile, hoping my acting was up to par this early in the morning.

Recently the town council had replaced the cracked sidewalks in town with old-fashioned boardwalks and had added wooden benches scattered in front of the shops. If you squinted some, you could imagine yourself back in the 1800s when the town was founded. I was pretty sure that was the council's plan, to attract tourists to our "quaint hamlet," as the Chamber of Commerce's brochure described it.

We settled on the bench nearest the sheriff's department. Not sure when his handler might show up, I got right to the point. "Avi, where were you the night Mary was attacked?"

"Like I told the police, home in bed, dreaming about her."

"And where's home?"

He grinned. "Now if I told you that, I'd have to kill you."

"Not funny," I said in a cranky voice. I am *not* normally an early riser. At least not this early.

He shook his head again, his face sobering. "I'm not supposed to give out my address unless I absolutely have to. I'm in a small apartment in DC."

"And your handler stays with you?"

"No. They wanted me to go into protective custody, but I resisted. I was supposed to stay in the apartment though, not go out at all. That got old."

"What are you doing for a living?"

"I work remotely, for several tech companies."

"Doing what?" I asked.

"Their bookkeeping. I can't use my CPA credentials right now, but I have a fake resumé saying I've been a bookkeeper for the past ten years."

"And what happens after this crooked producer goes to trial?"

"Depends on whether the feds get enough to convict the guy he was laundering money for. If everybody goes to jail, I can go back to my own life."

"Back in California."

He shook his head. "No. I'm thinking I'll stay in this area. I'm kinda sick of Hollywood."

Okay, enough beating around the bush. Time to find out if he was a psychopathic rapist.

"So, how did you happen to come down here to Virginia the very same day as Mary's attacker?"

"I figured she'd be down here with you, and I was afraid if I could figure that out, so could he. And I had to see her...see for myself that she was okay."

"But how did you know about my place down here? Mary said she never told you about it."

He gave me a strange look. "I remembered you were from Virginia."

Duh. Mary hadn't told X from the dating service about my place, but Avi, my old college chum, knew where I'd grown up.

"I checked the land records," he was saying, "and saw that you'd inherited your mom's house."

Hmm. That seemed like a lot of effort to find out where I lived.

"And you just *happened* to arrive around the time she was attacked again?" My tone dripped with disbelief. I was okay with that.

A black SUV cruised down deserted Main Street, going even slower than the posted twenty-five-mile limit. No doubt some tourists enjoying the "quaint" view. But I couldn't see inside as it slid past us. The passenger-side windows were tinted almost black.

Avi was shaking his head. "The sheriff told me about the attack." His hands had been lying on his khaki-clad thighs. Now he clenched his fists. "I can't believe the son of a bitch came after her again. But that was before the fire, right?"

I nodded.

"I saw smoke in the sky," he said, "as I approached your place. And heard the sirens. I pulled off to the side so I wouldn't be blocking emergency vehicles. I got out and ran toward the house. There were a bunch of firefighters gearing up. Then I saw Mary darting across your yard and going into the woods. I thought I saw someone go in after her, but I couldn't tell for sure. They were in the shadows under the trees. I took off–"

"Why didn't you tell the sheriff, instead of chasing her yourself?" I managed to keep the anger out of my voice. Hadn't the fool realized he'd scare the bejesus out of Mary?

"I saw his cruiser, gave that a moment's thought. But I was afraid he'd arrest me, and whether he did or not," his words were pouring out now, "precious time would be lost. I couldn't let the bastard catch her. He might not have only ra–" He choked on the word. "...assaulted her again. He might have *kidnapped* her." He swallowed hard, his Adam's apple bobbing in his throat.

I studied his face. He seemed genuinely upset at the memory. And putting myself in his shoes—assuming he wasn't the attacker himself—I probably would've done the same thing. I wouldn't stand around, waiting for the law to take over, when the woman I loved was at risk.

Something else was niggling at my brain. I shook my head, but the thought wouldn't step forward into the light.

I leaned a little to one side, trying to get a look at the back of Avi's head, to see if there was a lump or cut back there. But his hair was too thick.

"Do you have a headache today?" I asked.

"No." He gave me a funny look.

And the niggling thought darted out to center stage. "Wait! It was *you* parked on the shoulder? I almost hit your car as I was racing home."

Avi's forehead furrowed. "I thought I got it completely off on the grass, in your neighbor's yard."

"You didn't leave it up on the main road?"

He shook his head.

"The car on the road could've been the attacker's then." I jumped up. "It was gone this morning when I left the house."

The black SUV was cruising down the road the other way, going slightly faster than before.

Avi also stood. "Maybe the sheriff can find tire tracks."

"Where's your car?"

"One of the deputies drove it into town last night."

I nodded. *Good*, I thought, *and if your tires match the tracks up on the road, we'll know you're a liar.*

I glanced at Avi as I started toward the sheriff's department. He didn't seem nervous.

Movement out of the corner of my eye. I turned my head.

The SUV had slowed. The driver's side window was slightly open, a round pipe of some kind sticking out of it.

It registered what the pipe was as I heard the first crack. "Get down!" I yelled.

Another crack. A sharp pain in my arm, like a bee sting times a thousand.

A third gunshot, and Avi fell face down on the boardwalk.

CHAPTER ELEVEN

James

I stood over Avi, stunned.

"Get down yourself, you idiot!" he yelled. I dove to the boardwalk, landing half on top of him.

Tires squealed as the SUV sped off.

"What happened?" The sheriff's voice, shouting. "I heard shots."

I got to my feet. My right hand went to my stinging bicep. Something warm oozed between my fingers. My stomach roiled.

Avi was on his feet. "Black SUV," he huffed out. He was breathing heavily, hyperventilating.

"You're okay?" I heard the surprise in my voice. I'd been sure that he was hit.

He nodded, sucking in a deeper breath. "When you've feared for your life for months, you develop quick reflexes. Didn't catch the plate number. Did you?"

I shook my head, wincing.

Avi's gaze went to my bloody hand on my arm. "Lemme look at that." He shoved the short sleeve of my tee shirt up and poked at my bicep.

"Ouch." The stinging intensified. "Stop that."

"I don't think the bullet went in," he said. "It's just a graze."

The sheriff had stepped up, was peering over Avi's shoulder. "Yup, not too bad. Let's get inside in case the shooter circles back."

It had barely registered that two deputies had raced past us earlier and had jumped into a cruiser. Now I processed what they were doing. "You think your men will catch the guy?"

The sheriff shrugged and took my good arm to lead me to his door. Avi trailed behind, sticking close.

Inside his office again, the sheriff gestured toward his visitor chairs. He took a first aid kit from a cabinet and handed me a clean square of gauze. "You should go to the hospital."

I shook my head. The stinging had eased up some. And I had things to do today.

Some small part of my brain recognized that I'd gone numb. I wasn't feeling anything.

Sheriff Wallace frowned. "I'll call Doc an' see if he's available to assess how bad it is." He made that phone call, then turned back to us. "Now tell me what happened, from the beginning."

When we'd finished relaying everything we could remember about the SUV, he said to Avi, "You think it was that producer fella comin' after you?"

"Could be," Avi said, "but he would've hired a professional, and that professional would *not* have missed."

Wallace nodded. "Could be an incompetent professional. Not everybody's great at their job." He turned his gaze on me, icy blue eyes hard under his bushy eyebrows. "Or it could be Ms. Hanson's attacker, tryin' to get you to stop investigatin'."

I digested that, and another thought struck me. "Or it could be her attacker trying to take out Avi as competition for Mary's affections."

"So you believe me?" Relief was strong in Avi's voice.

"I'm leaning that way," I said. "That first attack, the guy went out of his way to make her think it was you. To know so much about her and about you, he had to have been stalking her for a while." I didn't say anything about what I'd learned from Fred, that Mary's attacker might have hacked into her office emails. I wanted to talk to Fred about that again, before mentioning it to anyone else. "He got to ra—"

Avi's blanching face stopped me from saying the word out loud.

"...to attack Mary, and turn her against you, all in the same act."

The sheriff nodded slowly. "Makes sense."

Back in my car, my arm bandaged up by the town's only doctor, I headed toward DC.

Doc had wanted to send me to the hospital two towns over for stitches. I'd declined, so he'd used a few butterfly bandages to close the wound, then wrapped it in gauze.

I still felt numb. Someone had shot at me, had wounded me even. Why wasn't I feeling *something* about that?

All these years I'd play-acted strong emotions on stage—had I grown impervious to real emotions? My stomach knotted and my head shook, as I downshifted in a curve.

I take that as a no, I thought.

So why wasn't I feeling anything...fear, horror, what?

I shuddered and decided not to look a gift horse in the mouth. I had things to do. I needed to figure out what was going on. For right now, I couldn't afford to feel.

My phone rang. I hit the answer button for the Bluetooth I'd retrofitted through my radio. It was the only upgrade I'd made to the classic Mustang.

"James," Mary's voice, "are you going into the city today?"

"Yes."

"Can you take me with you? I need some more clothes and I'd like to swing by my office, if that's okay, and touch base with Larry."

"Sure. I'll come get you." I made a U-turn in the middle of the deserted country road.

I didn't tell her that her workplace was exactly where I'd been headed.

I also failed to give any thought to Carrie's reaction to the big white bandage on my arm.

—•○•—

Mary

Carrie and I gasped in unison at the sight of James coming through the front door. Or more precisely, at the sight of the wide strip of white gauze wrapped around his upper arm.

We both jumped up from the sofa.

James glanced at us, then at the bandage. "It's only a graze."

"What happened?" Carrie said.

My heart was racing, dreading what new horror had occurred. But James just gave her a long, hard look.

She glared back. "Tell *us* what happened."

Her voice sounded angry. What was that about?

I felt slightly queasy. *I hope they're not having relationship problems.* It wouldn't be surprising if they were. This past year had been about as stressful as life gets. And now I'd brought my stress into their lives.

James shifted his gaze and sighed. "I went to see Avi at the sheriff's office. I wanted to talk to him before his handler whooshed him away to God knows where. We were sitting outside on a bench, which turned out to be a mistake."

He paused. "Someone shot at us, but he's fine."

My stomach churned as my mind scrambled to digest what he'd said. My mouth was hanging open, as was Carrie's. I clamped mine shut, swallowed hard. "Someone shot at you! Is Avi okay? You sure *you're* okay?"

"Yeah, although he might have a few bruises tomorrow. We both dove to the ground, and I landed on top of him."

"Who was shooting at you?" Carrie demanded.

He shook his head. "I don't know. It was a big black SUV, with tinted windows. All I saw was the barrel of a pistol sticking out, or at least I think it was a pistol."

"And you got hit." Carrie's tone softened. She gently touched the bandage.

"Just grazed. Doc Harvey patched me up. It shouldn't leave a scar."

Of course, he'd worry about that, being an actor. Out loud, I asked, "Was it the guy Avi's supposed to testify against?"

James shrugged and looked again at Carrie for a beat. "Could be, although he didn't think so. Also..." Another pause and glance at Carrie. "The sheriff thought it might be someone trying to scare me off from investigating."

Carrie said, "Maybe you should–"

"Hell no!" James half shouted.

Carrie pursed her lips and sucked in a big breath. "I was going to say maybe you should take my pistol with you, *when* you investigate."

"You don't want me to stop?"

"Yes." Her voice was anguished. "But no–" She stopped, shook her head. "Not if you don't think Avi is Mary's attacker. We can't keep living like this forever, not knowing who to trust."

"Why don't you think he's the attacker?" I asked.

"Long story," James said. "Short version. There was a car parked on the side of the road last night. I almost side-swiped it. Avi says it wasn't his, that he parked his rental on Carrie's yard, which is where the volunteer firefighters parked their cars."

He paused for breath. "The sheriff's sending deputies out to take casts both in the yard and where that car was on the road."

"So if Avi is telling the truth," Carrie said slowly, putting the pieces together as I was, "then his car's tracks will be in the yard, and the car on the road may be the attacker's."

Heat surged through my body. "And now," I said through gritted teeth, "he's an arsonist too." My chest hurt at the memory of that gaping black hole in James's house. "Guys, I am so sorry I brought this down on you."

Carrie's head jerked around toward me, her face pinched. Then her features softened. "Oh, sweetheart, none of this is your fault!"

Warmth spread through my chest. The ache was still there but... *You don't know how much those words mean to me.* But suddenly I was too shy to open my mouth, to say *those* words out loud to her.

Wind chimes tinkled sympathetically. Carrie and James didn't react. Maybe they were meant only for me this time. More warmth enveloped me.

James was shaking his head. "The sheriff said not to get our hopes up. The tracks most likely won't lead to who did it. They'll only provide some confirmation once there's a suspect."

He sighed. "I just can't see Avi as a rapist and arsonist. That's pretty sick, and he was always a fairly stable guy. Naive, but stable." James shook his head again. "He had a good childhood, I thought. I went to his house for Thanksgiving a couple of times in college, after the split with my parents. His folks were really nice."

A mix of hope and fear had me tensing again. Maybe Avi was a good guy after all. But could I really trust that?

Another thought popped into my head. "Wait, yesterday... Avi was wearing khakis and a button-down blue shirt. Not dressed all in black, like the attacker was." A wave of relief washed through me. "He couldn't have magically changed his clothes that fast, could he?"

James frowned. "He was still wearing those same clothes this morning, only rumpled from sleeping in them."

So why the skeptical expression?

"What was the attacker wearing exactly?" he asked.

"He was completely covered. Gloves, black windbreaker, the mask."

"And his pants?"

"Black as well." I closed my eyes, shuddered a little as I pictured him at the French doors. "But they were loose." My eyes flew open and I stared at James. "Like maybe a track suit?"

"So," Carrie said, her voice low and grim, "he could've had other clothes underneath."

My stomach bottomed out. I'd considered that myself yesterday, when I almost ran to one of the firefighters for help.

"Let's get going," James said. "We'll check your apartment, get your clothes and then go to your office."

"What did you need to do in DC?"

He got a strange look on his face and once again glanced at Carrie. "Talk to your friend Fred at your office."

"Why?" I asked, while wondering what the hell these two *weren't* saying out loud.

James sighed. "Fred thinks it's possible that someone hacked into your office email and saw the messages from Avi. They could've pieced together the things the attacker knew about you that way, from his end of your exchange."

Again my mouth was hanging open. I clamped it closed and tried to slow my pounding heart. I couldn't take this roller coaster of emotions much longer.

Then my chest tightened. "When exactly did you talk to Fred?"

"Yesterday, before my audition."

"And you're just now telling me about it?" My tense voice sounded strange to my own ears.

James flashed a guilty look in Carrie's direction. "Well, a lot was happening last night."

The tightening in my chest intensified. "I meant *before* you went to talk to him."

James held out his hands, palms up. "I'm sorry, Mare. Don't be mad. I should've told you."

"I'm not mad," I quickly said, but wondered if maybe I was.

I almost never got angry. Was that what the tightening in my chest was? Anger?

I shook my head slightly. "Come on," I said in a grim voice. "We need answers."

CHAPTER TWELVE

James

Once in my car, Mary asked, "What exactly did Fred say?"

"He actually hacked in there himself and pulled up those emails. It was kinda like listening to one side of a telephone conversation, but we could piece together enough. And if we could, so could your attacker."

Fred had texted me last night at some point, but in all the chaos I hadn't checked the message until much later. It said *May have found something. Can you come to town tomorrow?*

Rather cryptic, but it had been past midnight, too late to text back or call without waking him.

This morning, I'd realized that he might not be willing to say more in a text, or even a phone call. Just because you're paranoid, and all that. So I'd merely texted back that I'd be there by mid-morning.

Mary was nodding, her face pensive. "So it's someone who's good with computers."

"Beyond good. Someone with some serious hacking skills. And very likely someone from your job."

She looked at me, her eyes wide. "Fred and I are the only two people there who could do that."

"Hacking skills wouldn't necessarily be something a person would tell the world about."

"True."

I remembered the aftershave. "Hey, there's a small bag on the backseat. Can you reach it?"

She turned and stretched her arm back there. "Yeah, got it."

I hesitated. Would the scent give her an anxiety attack?

Then I flashed to the conversation with Carrie. Maybe it was time to stop protecting Mary's feelings so much.

She was holding the bag out toward me.

I didn't take it. "In the emails, X mentioned his brand of aftershave. I got some of it yesterday." I glanced sideways.

Her face had paled some, but she pulled the small bottle out of the bag, opened it and took a whiff.

Her face screwed up like she'd smell something disgusting. "Yes, that's what the attacker smelled like."

"And Avi, on your date?"

She nodded mutely and recapped the bottle. She began to roll down her window.

"Hey, what are you doing?"

"I...oh, sorry. I suddenly had this incredible urge to throw it out the window."

"Please don't. It was rather expensive."

"What are you going to do with it?"

I shrugged. "Maybe sell it on eBay."

She carefully slipped the bottle back in the Sephora's bag, and put it on the floor. Then she fell silent, staring out her side window at the passing scenery.

I was worrying that she was reliving the past few days.

"What was all that about with Carrie?" she said out of the blue. "Are you two having problems?"

I blew out air, half relieved, half dreading the change of subject. "Yeah, some, but I think it's only a rocky patch we're going through."

"What set it off? Unless you don't want to talk about it."

I decided to be honest with her, see what her take on it was. She was a pretty perceptive person.

"Carrie says I'm being too protective of you."

Mary tilted her head to one side. "Not now you're not."

"Well, now I'm being extra careful not to go there, especially in front of Carrie. But was I before?"

She shook her head slightly. "You were being very protective, but that felt good. It made me feel safer."

"That's what I told Carrie, that you were in no condition to make decisions for yourself right then."

I sensed her stiffen in the passenger's seat. "What?" I said.

She shook her head more vigorously. "I know it's not what you intended."

"Okay, but what did it sound like to you?" Maybe Mary could help me understand what Carrie was getting at.

"Just now, you sounded like Nick."

That hit me like a punch in the chest. "Your ex?" My voice squeaked some.

"He'd claim I was being overly emotional, and then he'd use that as an excuse to take charge, make decisions for me."

"In other words, control you."

She nodded.

"But you know that's not what I intended?"

"Yes, because I know you. But I am hyper-sensitive to those kinds of situations now."

"Apparently so is Carrie."

"Which is understandable," Mary said, "considering *her* history with an abusive spouse."

I thought about that. "This is just great. She's hyper-sensitive to control and I'm hyper-sensitive to criticism..." I trailed off, wondering why that was. An echo of that pressure in my chest from yesterday—and my thought at the time, that it was an *old* feeling.

"I'm afraid I got defensive with her," I said, "but we sorted it out."

What is that pressure about? Is it guilt?

Maybe because I knew Carrie was at least a little bit right.

No, it felt deeper than that...like I shouldn't even exist. I'd certainly gotten that vibe plenty of times from my stepfather. But it was my mother's frowning face that popped into my mind's eye.

After all I've sacrificed for you. One of her favorite lines when I'd done something to disappoint her. I now knew how truly horrific those sacrifices had been, but that knowledge didn't make the pressure go away.

If anything, it got worse.

"What's the feeling that goes even deeper than guilt?" I asked, then wondered why I'd said that out loud. It was a question I would've posed to Annaleise, but not to Mary.

But Annaleise is gone. My eyes stung.

"Goes deeper than guilt?" Mary echoed.

I nodded, my gaze on the road.

"Do you mean shame?"

The pressure in my chest was now crushing, but at the same time, my stomach relaxed. A feeling akin to relief spread through me. "Yeah, I think that's it." I swallowed hard.

How much more was I willing to share with Mary?

In for a penny, in for a pound. Annaleise's voice in my head. A memory, not her presence. We were too far from home.

"My mother had this look," I said, "when I'd done something wrong. It made me want to dig a hole, climb in, and then pull the dirt in on top of me."

Mary let out a short nervous laugh. "I know that look. And my former therapist would say that was definitely shame."

"What's the difference between that and guilt?"

"He said shame is about being, guilt is about behavior. And he said that guilt can be healthy, when it helps us recognize and change our 'maladaptive behavior.'" She made air quotes. "But shame, it only makes us feel bad about ourselves."

We both fell silent. The pressure had eased some. But I was grateful I was driving and had an excuse to stare straight ahead, not at Mary. Finally I said, "Does that stuff work?"

"What? Therapy? Yes, it really helped, after Nick left." She paused. "And I'm thinking I need to call my therapist again, get some help with..." She trailed off.

With the rape, I finished for her in my head.

She shook herself. "You've got to find the right person, though. Annaleise said it was like looking for a new car. It was a big investment so it was okay to test drive several counselors until I found one I trusted."

A lump formed in my throat and my eyes stung again. "Annaleise," I managed to push past the lump, "was wise beyond her years."

I saw Mary nod out of the corner of my eye. "She was an old soul. I'm sure she'd lived many lifetimes before this last one."

I glanced her way, cleared my throat. "You believe in all that?"

"Yes, I do."

"You weren't all that surprised when we told you about her ghost, were you?"

She shook her head. "Initial shock, yes, but then it made sense. Because of the way she died, and she–" Mary paused, turned more toward me in her seat. "She would've been worried about you, that her killer would go after you as well."

"Which he did, and if she hadn't been there to warn me and to help..." I trailed off, not sure how much to tell Mary. I'd always thought of her as fragile, especially since her divorce, but maybe... I shook my head slightly.

There was more to Mary than I'd thought—an inner strength I'd never given her credit for. No wonder she and Annaleise were friends. Annaleise would have seen that strength, that potential, and she wouldn't have been able to resist trying to bring it out.

An ache in my chest had replaced the lump in my throat. That's what Annaleise did, took on chicks with broken wings that she thought she could heal.

"Getting back to you and Carrie," Mary said, "my therapist would also say that awareness is half the battle."

I gave her a small smile. "Yeah, it is."

Mary didn't linger at her apartment. She grabbed some things out of her bedroom, while I checked the workmanship on the doorframe and locks.

"I thought you would take the time to change your clothes," I said when we were in the car again and headed for her office.

She shook her head and shuddered. "I had planned to, but..."

I grabbed her hand from her lap and gave it a squeeze, then quickly let go.

She didn't flinch this time.

I parked at the curb in front of her office building. Mary jumped out and fed the meter before I could get there.

As we both turned toward the building, a black Audi pulled into a reserved space, and Larry Bevans climbed out. He wore designer athletic shorts, expensive-looking sneakers, and a polo-style white shirt. A Washington Wizards cap perched on his head, a white tag sticking out the back of it.

I chuckled softly. The rest of his outfit was so meticulous.

"Hey, Mary," he yelled gleefully. He raced over and grabbed her in a bear hug.

She stiffened, but he still hung on. Finally he let her go, and she stepped back, looking a little shaken.

"Sorry," he said, "I guess I'm pretty smelly. Just came from a morning tennis match at the club." He grinned down at her. "It's great to see you. Are you coming back to work soon?"

She nodded. "In a day or two, if that's okay?"

"Sure. Of course. Whenever you're ready. I–"

He was cut off by screaming, coming from the side of the building.

Larry Bevans and I took off in that direction. We raced around the corner of the building.

Three women stood in a small courtyard. They were clutching coffee mugs, two of them still screaming. All of them were staring at something on the ground.

I followed their line of vision. The something was Fred Durham, lying on his back on the grass at the courtyard's edge.

His eyes were closed. *Why's he napping there?*

A breeze wafted my way, carrying a coppery scent. My stomach hollowed out.

I took a step forward. A dark red substance stained the grass around his head.

CHAPTER THIRTEEN

James

"What happened?" Larry Bevans yelled in the direction of the three women, now huddled together with shell-shocked expressions. One had a cell phone to her ear, calling 911.

"I thought I heard a thud," Larry said more quietly to me.

"Did you see him fall?" he yelled again at the women.

They shook their heads. "He was lying there," one of them said, her voice shaky. "When we came out for our coffee break."

I raced over and felt Fred's thick neck, searching for a pulse. Was that fluttering under my fingers? Maybe wishful thinking—the man didn't stir.

And a lot of blood had soaked into the grass. Some blades had turned a rusty brown. He hadn't just fallen a few seconds ago.

I wanted to *do* something, but I made myself step back. Moving him might do more harm.

Sobbing from behind me. *Mary!*

I jogged over to her and wrapped an arm around her shoulders. But I didn't go for a full hug, recalling her stiffness when Bevans had held her. Didn't he realize that a rape survivor might be uncomfortable with touch?

But did he even know about the rape? I'd been vague when I'd talked to him before. But she might've spoken to him since then.

Mary's shoulders had relaxed some under my arm, so I left it there.

Sirens in the distance, coming closer.

"You okay, Mare?"

"Yes," came out of her mouth, but she shook her head. Not surprising. Fred was a friend. Of course she was upset.

I gently pulled away, patted her arm. "I need to check something. Can you..."

She nodded.

I trotted over to the glass door leading into the building. Once inside I bolted up the fire stairs, two at a time, and ran to Fred's office. His door was sitting open.

I stopped in the doorway, scanned the room. The bins of computer parts that had been on the bookcase were now on the floor, the bits of metal and plastic scattered, as if someone had shoved them quickly off.

I had trouble visualizing Fred treating even a component of a computer that way.

The window was open. I took a step toward it and bumped the corner of the desk.

The two computer screens on it went from black to white. On one of them, stark against the white, were words in all caps: I'M SORRY, MARY. I'VE LOVED YOU FOR A LONG TIME. DIDN'T MEAN TO HURT YOU. CAN'T LIVE WITH MYSELF.

Fred was Mary's rapist? My brain couldn't wrap itself around that idea.

Sirens drawing closer jerked me out of my stunned state. I jogged back down the hall and fire stairs, coming out into the courtyard as the police and two paramedics came around the corner of the building.

I groaned. The detective trailing behind the uniformed officers was Talley, the jerk who'd questioned me and Mary in Paxtonburg.

I got to Mary as the uniforms were shooing her, Bevans and the women into the far corner of the courtyard. "No talking, please," one of the cops said.

The paramedics had gotten to work on Fred. I couldn't see him very well now—too many people were between us. But they'd braced his neck and had him on a back board. One was splinting his left arm while the other talked into a radio.

That flutter I'd felt, it must've truly been a pulse. If he were dead, they'd hardly be bothering with all that.

Bevans moaned from beside me. "What have I done?"

"What do you mean?" I whispered.

"I found out yesterday that he was hacking into other employees' email accounts. So I fired him."

"No talking," a nearby uniform barked.

A vise had tightened around my chest. I'd encouraged Fred to hack into Mary's account. Had I gotten him fired?

But what was with that message on his computer? Sure sounded like a suicide note. I shook my head slightly. Some things didn't jive here.

"Wouldn't security have escorted him out?" I asked in a low voice. "And changed his office's lock?"

Bevans shrugged and whispered, "I don't know how he ended up back in his office this morning."

The uniform glared at us.

An hour later, after we'd given our statements to an officer and had been instructed to come to the precinct for a more thorough interview that afternoon, we were allowed to leave.

Mary and I walked in silence to my car.

Once there, I told her about the note on Fred's computer and what Bevans had told me.

"I might've gotten him fired," I said, my throat so tight it was hard to get the words out. "My questions the other day prompted him to hack your account."

Mary was shaking her head slowly, her eyes wide.

"And I guess losing his job was the final straw," I added. My eyes stung.

Mary was now staring at me. "That note makes no sense. Fred couldn't have been the one who attacked me."

Mary

Detective Talley blew off my statement that Fred wasn't my attacker. "You said it all happened fast. You must've misjudged his appearance."

"Not *that* fast. He threw me on the bed at one point and then wandered around my room, touching..." I shuddered. "...my...things."

Movement out of the corner of my eye. James—who'd been sitting against the wall across the detectives' bullpen from Talley's desk—had risen from his chair. His expression was a mix of anger and worry.

I held up a hand in his direction.

He froze, stared for a beat, then nodded slightly and sat back down.

The detective shrugged. "A confession via suicide note is hard to dispute."

"What exactly did the note say?"

Talley consulted his notes and read out loud the words James had already told me. But I didn't want to get him in trouble for going up to Fred's office before the police arrived.

The words, *I didn't mean to hurt you,* sounded particularly off to me.

I shook my head. "Couldn't he have meant he didn't mean to hurt me by hacking into my private messages?"

He frowned, his eyes skeptical. "That's a stretch."

"So you're closing the case on my attack?"

"Not officially until the DNA results come back." He paused. "But essentially, yes."

His words were like a punch to the gut. I knew Fred was not my attacker, and now the bastard would be out there forever. And he could attack me again whenever he wanted.

And maybe worst of all, I didn't know whether or not I could trust X, aka Avi. I rubbed my breast plate with the heel of my hand, trying to ease the ache beneath it.

Somehow I managed to stand up. "Thank you for your time, Detective."

Talley's eyes softened some. "Take care of yourself, Ms. Hanson."

Resisting the urge to scream, I gave a slight nod and turned away.

James met me halfway across the room. He'd already given his formal statement to another detective. "What happened?" he whispered.

I shook my head and walked past him. I needed to get out of there before...

Once outside, I sucked in hot, humid air. Then I turned to James. "He's closed the case on my rape." My voice had a hard edge.

And it was the first time I'd used the R word since that night. Everyone, including myself, had been euphemistically calling it an *attack*. Which it was, but also much more.

I shuddered, and James moved to hug me. I held up a hand. "I'm okay. Let's get out of this damned city."

In his car, I asked, "Are you willing to keep investigating?"

James nodded. "I think we have to. You won't be safe until we find out who really attacked you."

"And now we have another reason, to avenge the attack on Fred." Again, that hard edge in my tone. Pressure in my chest made me sit up straighter in the passenger seat.

I realized I was pissed. Yes, this was what anger felt like. And it felt good, strong.

James glanced my way, then back to the road. "You don't believe the note then?"

"Not for a New York minute. Fred might have had a crush on me. And it might not have been the first time he hacked into my account–"

"He did seem to do so pretty easily," James interrupted. "I just thought at the time that he had great geek skills."

"He did...he does." I swallowed hard. "The detective said he wasn't dead, but he's in bad shape."

James nodded again, his lips pressed together in a thin line.

"Anyway," I went on, "I don't believe Fred attacked me. He's not the right height and build. And I don't think he has it in him."

"He seems like a nice guy," James said.

"He's a sweetheart."

We were quiet for a couple of minutes. The crowded streets and tall buildings of the city segued into somewhat less daunting suburbs.

James glanced my way again. "You know what this means, don't you?"

"The rapist tried to frame him," I said, then pushed out through gritted teeth, "which makes it even more likely that it's someone I work with."

"And," James said, his eyes back on the road, "he was trying to kill Fred. He's escalating."

CHAPTER FOURTEEN

James

Mary had fallen silent, staring out the side window—apparently absorbed in her own thoughts.

Meanwhile, my brain kept going around in circles, trying to come up with a new angle to investigate. With no results except a growing sense of panic.

We were about halfway home when Mary stirred. "You knew Avi in college. What was he like then?"

I glanced her way. Her face was turned toward me, her expression an odd mixture of wary and hopeful.

Good Lord, this must be confusing as hell for her, not knowing if she can trust this guy or not.

"He was naive," I said out loud, then paused, thinking back. "Well, we were all naive then, but with Avi, it was more of a personality trait." I chuckled softly.

"What do you mean?"

"I guess that he's an eternal optimist. He always believes everything will turn out okay."

She smiled a little. "Not a bad trait to have."

"Yeah, I guess. I mean it's probably preferable to my darker view of the world."

"But you're the one who succeeded as an actor," Mary said.

I chuckled again. "Well, let's just say, his parents were smart to make him finish getting his degree in accounting."

"He wasn't that good at acting."

"No, but he loved it, so the drama club advisor gave him mostly the comic parts. He could pull those off okay."

She nodded, then muttered under her breath, "I could use a bit more optimism right now."

Not sure what to say to that, I didn't respond.

She turned back toward her window, again leaving me alone with my thoughts.

I tried to focus on the scenery, and the feel of the Mustang's powerful engine—something that usually put a smile on my face—as we zipped along the country roads.

It didn't work. The anxiety about the investigation was creeping back.

Before, I'd considered my efforts as supplementing the law enforcement agencies who were investigating. But now the DC police had closed Mary's case, believing that Fred had been her attacker. And the Feds protecting Avi seemed content to assume all would be well, if they could only keep him under wraps until the trial.

Who knew where Sheriff Wallace stood? Was he also assuming that the shooter this morning had been after Avi, and therefore it was not something his department needed to investigate?

Maybe I needed to drive into town and have a sit-down with the good ole boy. Because I was leaning toward Avi's interpretation, that the shooter was trying to dissuade me from continuing to investigate Mary's attack.

And I probably should stop. I didn't really know what I was doing. I didn't have any training or skills as an investigator. Yes, I'd been a party to solving three murders before—well five, if you counted the collateral damage. But I'd mostly been on the defensive in those cases, waiting until the culprits showed themselves and then doing my best to bring them down.

With Carrie's help in both cases. My chest warmed.

I couldn't take that approach this time. This rapist didn't seem willing to just wait until he got a crack at Mary again. He was trying to smoke her out, literally.

And he'd damaged my house trying, and now Carrie and her son were at risk too.

How could I protect all of them? I heard a soft keening sound and glanced over at Mary.

She was looking out the side window, didn't seem to be making any noise.

With a jolt, I realized the sound had come from me. My stomach was churning with anxiety. I needed to be more proactive in the investigation, yet I had no idea what to do next. Fred had been the source of my best lead, but now he was out of commission.

What am I going to do, Annaleise?

No response.

Were we still too far from the house for her to hear me...or connect with me...or whatever the hell she did? I had no idea how far she was able to roam. She'd shown up in the nearby woods a time or two, and at Carrie's house.

I really didn't know that much about ghosts. Indeed, I knew about as much about ghosts as I did about investigating.

Annaleise... My chest ached. It had been almost nine months and I still missed her like crazy. She had been my best friend for almost twenty years. We'd known each other so well, had always had each others' backs.

But I wasn't there when she needed me most. When she should've been safe, in *my* house! But she wasn't.

The coppery smell invaded my nose. Rusty red streaks and splatters across a sunny yellow wall.

A warm hand on my arm. I jumped.

"James, pull over. Let me drive."

"Wha'?" I glanced over. "Why?"

Mary's face was ashen. "Pull over, James! You're driving erratically."

My head swiveled back to the front. The tree-lined country road was dappled with sunlight. But the image was kind of blurry. I carefully slowed and eased the car onto the shoulder, put it in park.

Mary got out to jog around to my side of the car.

I skimmed the back of my hand across my cheek. It came away wet.

Mary opened my door.

I managed to get out and make my way to the passenger side. Settling back in that seat, I tried to relax my tense muscles, with only partial success.

Mary pulled out onto the road.

As we drew closer to the turnoff leading to my house and Carrie's, my eyes began to sting and my chest felt like a vise was squeezing it. I opened my mouth, gasping some for air.

"Are you alright?" Mary asked, keeping her eyes on the road as we approached the gravel drive.

"Yes," I lied, while thinking, *What the hell's the matter with me?*

Then the tinkle of wind chimes, and a warmth slowly enveloped me. My muscles went limp.

I can't let you go, Annaleise.

The wind chimes sounded again, tinkling out a four-beat rhythm. *You don't have to. You don't have to.*

Carrie

Mary's words kept echoing in my head. *Poor Annaleise. We have to help her.*

She was right.

But maybe it hadn't been my best move to bring up helping Annaleise move on—into the light, or whatever—tonight.

James seemed off somehow. He was pacing the floor of my small kitchen.

"Are you okay?" I asked.

"Yeah." He shook his head. "Now is not the time."

And for you, it may never be. That thought came unbidden into my mind.

Not for the first time, I wondered if James had been in love with Annaleise. He'd said no, when I'd asked him once. They were only platonic friends. But...

Was I jealous of a ghost?

The soft tinkle of wind chimes, as if Annaleise were trying to reassure me.

I hid a smile. James would want to know what it was about, and I was not willing to share these particular thoughts.

"For one thing," he was saying, "we need her help right now. She's better than a burglar alarm."

"This is true," I said. "So let's talk about how we're going to protect ourselves from this crazy guy who's after Mary.

How do we keep him from burning down this house, with us in it."

James stopped pacing, dropped into the chair across from me at the table, and put his head in his hands. "I don't know."

I sighed. "Well, hopefully Annaleise and/or Ginger will warn us if he gets close to the house."

James lifted his head. "And he didn't burn my house until Mary had left, had come over here. He doesn't want to hurt her...Um, I mean, at least, he doesn't want her dead."

"No," I spat out, "he wants to own her." I was a little surprised by the vehemence in my voice. "Sometimes I wonder how truly civilized we humans are. There are way too many men who still think it's okay to grab the woman by the hair and drag her off to his cave."

James grunted.

Which struck me funny. This time I didn't bother to hide my smile.

He looked at me, held my gaze, and slowly a matching smile spread across his face. "Well, I may still grunt but I refuse to live in a cave. And I'm not dragging you anywhere. You're too heavy."

"Hey, watch it, Bub." I mock swatted his arm, while chuckling.

Phillip chose that moment to come in the back door. "Hey, what are you guys laughing about?"

I smiled at him. "Just having a light moment, as we try to figure out what to do to keep us all safe tonight."

"I've been thinking about that," Phillip said. "I think we should set up a booby trap. I've actually started on it."

"What?" James and I said in unison.

"I'm digging a trench on our side of the back fence."

We had recently installed a six-foot fence around my backyard, so we could let Ginger out there to do her business. I'd had an electronic invisible fence to keep her on the property before, but it had stopped working. So I'd convinced my landlord a privacy fence would be a valuable improvement. He'd paid for the materials, and Phillip and I had put it up.

I knew the fence was scalable, but I felt more secure with it there. It had only one gate, which we kept padlocked from the inside at night.

"I know we've got Ginger and the alarm system," Phillip's excited words rushed out, "but it would be good to know someone is coming before they get close to the house. If this guy jumps the fence, he'll land in the ditch." He paused for a minuscule breath. "I'm gonna put a string of tin cans along the other edge of the ditch, so when he tries to climb out, we're alerted. That's what I came in for, the recycle bin."

James was grinning at me. "Smart kid you got. It might just work." He pulled the bin of recyclables out from under the sink. "There's more things we can use in my garage. Come on, I'll help you dig." James headed for the back door.

I tried not to laugh out loud as my two guys went off to dig in the dirt.

<hr />

James

I'd gone along with Phillip's idea on a whim. Who knew if it would work, but I had no better way to fill the time until dinner. I should be trying to figure out where to go next in my investigation. But my brain kept veering back to that strange episode while driving home this afternoon.

Was it only grief for Annaleise? It had almost felt like a flashback.

I shook my head. Maybe some mind-numbing physical labor would give my subconscious mind a chance to think of something new to try in the investigation.

That often worked when I was stuck on how to handle a certain scene in a play. I'd volunteer to help build or paint props and let the problem percolate in the back of my mind.

With one arm injured, I wasn't keeping up with Phillip very well. I could only lift small shovels full of dirt.

He swiped sweat off of his face with the back of an arm and managed to leave a dark streak of dirt across his forehead.

I suppressed a smile. A strange pressure was building in my chest as we worked, not unpleasant but also not familiar.

With a jolt, I realized it was pride...in Phillip. He really was a smart kid, and resilient. Carrie had done a good job raising him, despite her ex's poor role model.

I had grown fond of Phillip, but otherwise I hadn't given my relationship with him all that much thought. Well, at one point early on, I had told him I wasn't trying to replace his father, but I wanted to be his friend. I'd said that mostly to win his approval of my relationship with his mother. It seemed the right tone to set.

I shoveled some more dirt out of the ditch, then stopped and wiped sweat off my own face with the hem of my t-shirt.

Phillip held up a length of heavy-duty twine, with several cans and bottles tied to it. "Do you think these are close enough together?"

I nodded, distracted by another swell of pride in my chest.

Pride was more a paternal feeling, wasn't it? Was I starting to think of him as a son?

I shook my head slightly and went back to shoveling, keeping my head down. My face felt flushed with something more than the summer heat.

Where was my relationship with Carrie going?

Good question. So far, it had lasted nine months, about three times as long as my romances usually did.

Was that because I didn't have the comfort of my friendship with Annaleise to run back to, when things got sticky?

Not completely. Carrie was different. I really wanted this to last, but I didn't dare trust that it would be forever.

I was working harder at this relationship than ever before. Trying to sort out my feelings when things got tense, instead of just spewing them all over her. The latter strategy had not worked out well in the past. Defensiveness had led to anger, and that to more anger, and then to rejection. More often me rejecting than being rejected.

But Carrie and I had not talked about long-term commitment much. We did say "I love you," to each other. Another step that I'd never taken before—and actually meant it, that is.

And I'd said some things—after Phillip had shown up and we'd known his father wouldn't be far behind—about being "in this together." I may have even used the word *committed* to "seeing it through together."

Around that time, she had legally named me as Phillip's guardian, should something happen to her. It was a matter of expediency then, since she was looking at the possibility of going to prison, and her ex's new girlfriend was suing for custody of the boy, to get control of his father's business and money.

But what if something happened to her? That thought set off an anxious shudder deep in my core. Was it about losing her, or about the responsibility for Phillip? Probably both. What the hell did I know about being a father?

Speaking of lousy role models, mine had been my stepfather, an obnoxious man on his best day, who did not like children and seemed to hate me in particular.

"Hey, James." Phillip's voice broke into my thoughts. "We're gonna run out of string. You got any at your house?"

"Sure." I gave him a fake smile. "I'll get it."

I let myself out of the gate and headed across the grassy strip of land between the houses. My footfalls were heavy, trying to stomp my anxious thoughts into the ground.

Mary

At dinner, I kept my head down. It was cramped around Carrie's small kitchen table. And I was beginning to feel bad for sponging off Carrie and James for so long.

My phone buzzed. I glanced down at it in my lap but didn't recognize the number. It buzzed again. I should ignore it, but some instinct said to answer it.

"Excuse me," I mumbled and jumped up from the table. I wasn't really hungry anyway.

Once out of the kitchen, I answered. "Hello?"

"Mary, please don't hang up. It's me, Paul."

"Paul?"

"Oh, I'm sorry. That's my middle name. I use it for business. It's X."

Suddenly, all his craziness with different names rankled. "I prefer Avi." My tone was snappish.

I started to feel guilty, but told myself not to go there. I had every right in the world to be annoyed with this guy.

"Honestly, I prefer that too," he said. "I think I'm going to go by Avi from now on, at least socially."

I didn't say anything as I headed for the stairs and my room.

After a beat, he said, "I just wanted to apologize again for chasing you in the woods. It didn't dawn on me at first that you'd assume I was your attacker. I thought he was after you."

"I thought he was too," I shot back.

A pause. "I saw shadows moving, under the trees. I was trying to get to you before he did, to protect you. But maybe... Now that I think about it, they could've been branches blowing in the breeze, the shadows I mean."

"Or maybe he was after me, and you scared him off." Then something occurred to me. "Did you run past where I was hiding in that thicket, and then circle back?"

"No. I was running after you, and suddenly you were there in front of me. I grabbed you partly to keep from knocking you down."

So the dark shadow that ran past my hiding place could've been the real attacker. Or Avi could be lying.

I shook my head. *Damn!* I didn't know what to believe.

I let my frustration fuel my courage. "Avi, did you hurt Fred?"

"Fred? Who's Fred?"

"A colleague of mine, and a friend," I said, my mind searching for a way to tell, one way or the other, if Avi was being truthful.

"What happened to him?"

"He fell out of his third-floor office window."

"Oh my God!" Avi exclaimed. "I'm sorry, Mary. Were you really close?"

I had an idea. "Yes, he was a good friend. Um, the funeral's tomorrow."

"I wish I could be there to support you."

"When does the trial begin?" I asked, a bit absentmindedly. Most of my brain cells were focused on processing that Avi didn't know that Fred was still alive. Did that mean he was the one who tried to kill Fred, and he was assuming he'd succeeded?

Or did it only mean that Avi was isolated enough right now that he didn't know what was happening in the outside world?

Had what happened to Fred even made it onto the evening news? In DC, somebody got hurt or killed at least once a day—more like several somebodies. Plus there was all the political news.

Someone jumping out a window, and ending up in a coma, might not even get a spot on the evening broadcasts. My chest deflated. My ploy of pretending that Fred had died had netted me nothing.

I tuned back in as Avi was saying, "...can't wait for it to be over."

Damn, I'd missed the answer to my question. "Uh, me either."

"Maybe I could sneak out in disguise, and meet you at the funeral?"

My heart jumped into my throat. "No! It's too dangerous." I swallowed hard, a little surprised at the intensity of my fear for his safety.

"Is it even safe for you to be calling me?" I asked.

"What my handler doesn't know won't hurt me," he quipped.

"Yeah, but can the guy you're going to testify against track your phone?"

"No, it's a disposable."

It dawned on me that it was safer for Fred if people did believe he was dead. "I... I'll be okay, at the funeral. You can't take the risk that someone will try to shoot you again."

"I'm not convinced they were aiming at me. I'm afraid for James—that it was whoever attacked you, trying to get him to back off."

"I'm worried about him too."

"He *should* back off and let the authorities handle it," Avi said.

I had no idea how to respond to that. Was he saying that only out of concern for James, or did he have another motive?

I didn't want to tell him that James *couldn't* back off. None of us were safe until my attacker was behind bars.

And Avi could be that attacker. I wasn't convinced that he wasn't. And I didn't want to let him know that I was now fair game, because the police had decided the case was solved.

I'd reached my room. Closing the door, I sat on the side of my bed.

A vise closed around my chest, making it hard to breathe. My eyes stung. I'd already been half in love with this guy before that first date.

I shook my head, admitting to myself that I'd fallen the rest of the way in love when he'd kissed me that night. I'd thought he was the sweetest guy ever.

Until I'd thought he was the one who'd raped me!

A tear drop landed on my arm. A sob was trying its damnedest to escape from my throat. But I couldn't let him hear me crying. He'd want to know why.

I didn't want to tell him that I loved and feared him, pretty much in equal measure.

"Well, it's getting late," Avi said, sounding awkward. "I should let you go so you can get some sleep."

"Okay," I managed to choke out, while swiping at my wet cheeks with the back of my hand. "Um, goodnight."

"Goodnight, sweetheart." He disconnected.

My chest warmed at the *sweetheart*, even as my stomach roiled. I let the sobs come.

CHAPTER FIFTEEN

Carrie

Halfway through dinner, Phillip paused in the act of shoveling food into his mouth and looked at each of us in turn. "So, I guess the fire at James's house has kinda forced the issue, huh?"

"What issue?" I asked.

"You two are finally cohabitating." He gave us a big grin.

"No, we're not," I said, perhaps too quickly.

The grin held. "You're not? Might as well be. You haven't been fooling me at all, ya know. I know you sleep together almost every night."

I shook my head slightly. "And you're okay with that?"

"Yeah. Why wouldn't I be?" Phillip tilted his head toward James. "He's a nice guy, and he makes you happy."

I felt the corners of my mouth quirking upward. I glanced at James, but he was staring down at his plate. "And there you have it," I said, "short and simple."

"It's kind of an odd time to be making that decision," James said. Then he looked from me to Phillip and back again. "But I guess we are...basically cohabitating."

We're living together. Warmth spread through me at the thought, but butterflies had invaded my stomach.

James's expression was neutral. He didn't seem all that excited about the idea.

I covered his left hand, lying on the table, with my own. "I guess we are then." I smiled.

He put his fork down.

I glanced at his plate, still two-thirds full. "Done so soon?"

"I'm not very hungry tonight." He paused. "Just worried about things."

A small spurt of annoyance. I let go of his hand. I was worried about our safety too, but we could take a moment to be happy about this, couldn't we?

As soon as the dinner dishes were cleared, Phillip excused himself and went off to his room to play video games.

"He does that an awful lot," James said, while rinsing the dishes. "Is it all that healthy?"

I shrugged and took a plate to load in the dishwasher. "He's still recovering from losing his father, so I'm not going to get on him for it right now. It distracts him, if nothing else."

James nodded. "Maybe we could get him involved in some sports at the high school this fall? I think the public schools let home-schooled kids participate in them."

I took another plate from him. "Good idea."

The tension in my stomach and chest relaxed some. He'd said *we*. It sounded like he was accepting the idea that we were now a committed couple.

But still his reactions were a little odd. He seemed preoccupied.

Was it too soon to bring up the next step? Or what *I* thought the next step should be.

James

Thoughts of the strange feelings this afternoon tried to invade my mind. I quickly shoved them aside, focusing on what sports might be best for Phillip. He wasn't big enough to play football, but maybe basketball or soccer?

"James, what's the matter?"

"Nothing," I said, too quickly. My heart rate jumped up a notch.

Carrie shook her head. "You've been off all afternoon. Something's going on."

She closed the dishwasher, hit the buttons, and busied herself with putting on the kettle for her evening dose of chamomile tea.

I was grateful for the time to gather my thoughts. How much was I willing to tell her?

Another thought gave me pause. Mary might say something to her.

"I, uh, think I might be coming down with something," I lied.

She turned toward me, mug and teaspoon in her hands. "Do you have a fever?"

I shook my head. "No, I, um, just felt kind of weird this afternoon. But I was driving, which made it kind of scary." I didn't want to tell her it had started with grief over Annaleise, then had morphed into...whatever it was. "Mary made me pull over, and she drove the rest of the way home."

Carrie's expression was anxious. "Maybe you should go see the doctor."

I shrugged. "I will, if it happens again."

The kettle whistled, and she turned to pour her tea. "We've been under a lot of stress lately."

I faked a chuckle. "Yeah, you could say that."

Carrie gestured toward the kitchen table. We sat down across from each other.

She took a small sip of tea, then paused with the cup still near her lips. "James, I think we should move."

"Wha'? Move what?"

"House." She put her cup down. "I think we should live somewhere else."

I didn't answer, just stared at her. A jumble of feelings swirled in my chest and stomach.

"I'm almost finished the renovations on this house," she continued. "The front porch is the last project, and I'll start on that tomorrow. And I think you need to get away from your house." She tilted her head in that direction.

"You want me to *sell* the house?"

And leave Annaleise? My heart raced even faster.

"No, you don't have to sell it, not until you're ready. But I will have to move soon. And–"

"You and Phillip can move in with me. There's plenty of room. It's a big house." I heard the desperation in my voice. My cheeks heated.

"But it's going to take a couple of months for the contractor to repair the fire damage." Carrie's tone was gentle, her eyes warm and worried. "And I don't think it's healthy for you to be living there now. Too many bad memories."

She paused again, drew in a deep breath. "I *know* I don't want to live there. James, we killed a man in that house."

"Because he was trying to kill us!"

"I know, and I don't feel all that guilty about it. But every time I walk through the living room—" She stopped, shuddered a little.

"I'm going to enroll Phillip in the high school in Paxtonburg in the fall," she continued. "I was only home-schooling to help him get caught up—from the time he lost when he ran away from his dad and was looking for me. But he needs to be around kids his own age. So I'd like to live closer to town. Not in town but..."

"But what?" I said, hoping she would keep talking long enough for me to sort out the churning in my stomach and the panicky feeling in my chest.

She stared at me, her eyes shiny. "I want to be part of a community again. The close-knit neighborhood where I grew up, that's what saved me as a kid, living with my crazy mother. I could go to a neighbor's house when she went on a rampage. I haven't had that kind of support for years. First Greg isolated me from my friends, and then I was in hiding..." She trailed off again. "I want to have a normal family, in a normal home, in a normal neighborhood. Is that too much to ask?"

"It is if I have to leave Annaleise," I blurted out. The swirling feelings had eased, but the pressure in my chest was intense.

Carrie had frozen in the act of lifting her cup to her mouth. She slowly put it back down. "You were in love with her," she said, a statement not a question. But there was no rancor in her voice.

My heart felt like it would explode. My throat hurt. "Ye–" I started to say, then choked on the word. My shoulders were shaking. I squeezed my eyes shut, trying to block out the feelings.

The scrape of a chair, the fluttering of clothing next to my arm. Carrie gathered me to her, held my head against her warm breast. She stroked my hair.

My body tingled, the beginnings of arousal. I wanted to relax in her arms, let her soothe at least some of the pain and grief away.

She kissed my forehead and let her face linger close to mine. It was an invitation. My body longed to accept it, to kiss her, to make love to her.

A new kind of pain in my heart. I *did* love this woman. I absolutely didn't want to lose her. I even loved her son. But...

I felt myself going cold in her arms, my heart closing off—the way it had been, before Carrie. For so many years, I'd only dated casually, pretending I was incapable of love, all the while loving Annaleise. Because she was safe, a friend. A *married* friend at that.

I pulled away from Carrie and stood up. "I can't talk about this anymore tonight. We've got to focus on staying safe."

"Of course, I–"

I turned away, toward the door to the living room.

"Where are you going?" There was a touch of panic in her voice.

It felt like a knife through my chest. I knew I was hurting her. But I couldn't manage to form any words of reassurance. Instead I said, in as neutral a tone as I could muster, "To get a sheet and pillow. I'm sleeping on the sofa again, in case this bastard tries to break in tonight."

I paused in the doorway. The pain and anxiety in her eyes were almost more than I could bear.

"Okay." She swallowed hard. "We don't have to decide anything tonight." Her voice caught a little as she added, "I do love you, James."

"I know," I pushed past the lump in my throat. But I couldn't make the words, *I love you too,* come out.

I finally managed, "Me too." And I left the room.

CHAPTER SIXTEEN

Carrie

I lay in bed, staring at the ceiling.

What had I been thinking, pushing James like that to move? I knew he had trust issues. I should've let him digest the idea of living together for a while.

I didn't have to tell my landlord right away that the house was done; I could buy us a couple of months.

What if James leaves me? Panicky butterflies ping-ponged inside my chest. The old sick, hollow feeling settled in my stomach. The feeling I'd had every night for years, as I'd cried myself to sleep, missing my father, and feeling totally alone.

Get a grip, woman, I told myself. I wasn't an abandoned teenager anymore. I could take care of myself.

I'd proven that when I'd left Greg and come to Virginia, found this house, negotiated with the landlord. It had been lonely at first, but I'd gotten used to it.

And now I had Phillip back with me, so I wouldn't be alone, at least not for a few years yet. Eventually he'd leave for college.

I rolled over and punched my pillow. Why was love so damned complicated?

James

After a semi-sleepless night, I snuck out of the house early, to go see Sheriff Wallace.

As I parallel-parked in front of his department, my left bicep was throbbing, letting me know that digging ditches when wounded was not the best idea. I was hoping there wasn't any permanent damage. Physical handicaps could limit the roles an actor was offered. Not that I'd ever been the he-man type, even though I tried to stay in shape.

Sharp rapping, next to my ear. I jumped in the driver's seat.

Sheriff Wallace himself was standing outside my window. I lowered it.

"Is there a reason, son, why you're parked in my space?"

"Oh, sorry. I'll move the—"

He waved his hand in the air. "Never mind. Were ya comin' to see me?"

"Yes." I turned off the engine and climbed out of the Mustang.

The sheriff ran an admiring eye over the car. "She's a beauty."

I managed a small grin. "Thanks. It's all that's left of my player days."

He grinned back. "Ms. Carrie's got ya settlin' down, does she?"

"Yeah." I said, suddenly uncomfortable with the topic, even though I'd brought it up.

Do I really want to go back to my player days? The answer was, not really. I did love Carrie, but the old restlessness was kicking in. Or maybe that was nerves because of what was going on.

I followed Wallace into the building. He waved me to a chair by his desk and offered coffee.

I gratefully accepted. It was quite good, belying the stereotype that cop-house coffee is always terrible.

He took a big sip from his own cup, sighed loudly, then put the mug down on his desk. "Now, what can I do for you today, James?"

I told him about what had happened to Fred, including about the note on his computer, that the DC police were interpreting as both a suicide note and a confession that he'd sexually assaulted Mary. "They've closed the case, but we're not at all convinced that Fred was her attacker. And now we're feeling really vulnerable. Whoever *did* attack her could come after any of us at any time."

"Not on my watch," the sheriff growled.

At first, I thought he meant it wasn't his problem. My heart sank into my stomach.

But he shook his head. "They may have closed their case, but I still have an arson and a shootin' to investigate."

I downright sagged in my chair, as the tension left my body.

"Harumph, do you really have that low an opinion of my little department? You didn't think we'd keep after those cases?"

"No, no, I just..." I trailed off, not sure what I had thought. Of course he would keep investigating. Even if Fred was responsible for all of it—the attack, the arson and the shooting—the sheriff would want to know that for sure.

I blew out air. "I guess I've been so focused on how to protect Carrie and Mary, and Phillip."

"I understand," Wallace said. "You've taken quite a burden on your shoulders."

"Do I have a choice?"

"Well, technically you do, but I think most men would be doin' what you're doin', under the circumstances."

"Carrie thinks maybe I shouldn't have brought Mary down here from DC in the first place."

Wallace raised a bushy sandy-gray eyebrow. "What other choice was there?"

"I could've taken her to a hotel, or my apartment in the city." My place was small, with only one bedroom, but I could've slept on the couch, keeping Mary safe but not jeopardizing Carrie and Phillip.

I shook my head. "I guess hindsight is always twenty-twenty, huh?"

"Yup."

"So, where do we go from here?" I asked.

"*You* don't go anywhere," the sheriff said. "You stay home and protect everybody, to the best of your ability. I've already got a deputy patrollin' that road in front of your property. And one'll be parkin' in your driveway at night. Me and the rest of my boys will be doin' the investigatin'."

His "boys" included two female deputies, but I opted not to point that out.

Wallace liked to pretend he was only a good ole boy sheriff, maybe not too bright, and certainly not very modern. But it was mostly an act, designed to get the bad guys to underestimate him.

"The problem is," I said, "that all this ties in with Mary's attack, and that happened in DC, which is out of your jurisdiction. And she and I think it may be someone she works with, someone who knew she and Fred were friends."

"Just because it's out of my jurisdiction don't mean I can't have my people talk to folks up there."

Despite the efforts of the sheriff to convince me I should leave things to him, my brain was still trying to figure out the next step in the investigation. "But if you go into the law firm, in uniform, people are gonna be a lot more defensive than if I'm asking questions."

"*Or* they'll feel more compelled to answer my questions, and truthfully, since I'm the law, even if it ain't my jurisdiction. Law enforcement agencies cooperate. I can git the local police to help me out if need be." He paused for half a beat. "And may I point out that you're a civilian."

I ignored that last part. "If you all go in there, the bastard might get too scared and lay low for a while. Then we'd never know when he would resurface and come after Mary again."

"Son, you're overthinkin' this."

"Probably." I stared at the sheriff for a moment. I'd been terrified of him when I'd first met him, since I was initially his prime suspect in Annaleise's and Charles's murders.

And now this guy was sitting here, letting me drink his coffee, and patiently discussing the case with me, more or less.

Warmth slowly filled my chest. "I *do* have a tendency to overthink things," I admitted.

He chuckled softly. "Ya think?"

I smiled at the pun and leaned forward. "How about this? One of your people goes with me, undercover, maybe posing as a private detective that I've hired. I'm on good terms with Mary's boss. I'm pretty sure he'd let me question the staff, even though I'm not law enforcement. That way, if we discover something, your man can make an arrest, and if I get into trouble, he'll be there to protect me."

The sheriff was silent for a full beat. I suspected he was only humoring me, pretending to think about what I'd said, before politely but firmly kicking me out of his office.

"Ya know, son, that plan may have merit."

I almost fell off my chair.

Wallace put his big hands on his desk and pushed himself to a stand. "Only it won't be one of my deputies goin' with ya. It'll be me."

Mary

I laid down for a nap. I'd hardly slept at all last night, or any night for that matter, since the attack. Every night had been riddled with nightmares, full of fear, fire, running through the woods.

At one a.m., I'd taken some melatonin, concerned that a stronger sleep aid might keep me asleep, trapped in a bad dream. It had only helped a little. I'd dozed on and off until dawn, and I'd felt groggy ever since.

I was drifting in and out, occasionally hearing the whir of Carrie's sander. She'd gotten cheap rent on the house, in exchange for fixing it up for sale. The interior was done now, so she'd tackled the front porch today, sanding down the peeling paint on the floorboards and railings.

I pulled my pillow over my head, trying to block out the noise.

I was starting to drift off. Ginger's muffled barking. I clasped the pillow tighter against my ear.

The whine of the sander dimmed as sleep tugged me downward. The faint sound of wind chimes.

A scream. *Oh shit, here comes another nightmare.*

CHAPTER SEVENTEEN

James

We hadn't called ahead. The sheriff preferred the element of surprise. "And if the big boss ain't there," he'd said, "we'll come back when he is. Y'all can take me to one of them fancy restaurants in DC, while we wait." Then he'd changed into his "civvies," as he called them. Black jeans, a blue polo shirt that matched his eyes, and a Washington Nationals baseball cap.

"I got one for every jurisdiction 'round here." He tapped the hat's brim as we walked out the back of the building and over to a white, unmarked SUV. "Baltimore Orioles, Pittsburgh Pirates, and the Phillies. Even got a West Virginia Mountaineers' cap. If nothin' else, they're a great conversation starter."

We were mostly quiet during the long drive to DC. The discussion of his baseball cap collection seemed to use up Wallace's quota of small talk.

My thoughts wandered—and landed on the conversation with Carrie over moving. Apparently, she had already been thinking about the cohabitating thing before Phillip brought it up.

I wasn't sure how I felt about that. On the one hand, the thought of living together, the three of us being a true family, made my chest warm.

But resentment niggled around the edges of that warmth. Was Carrie taking long-term commitment as a given in our relationship? Early on, in the first blush of love, we'd discussed the fact that two big houses, plus my apartment in DC, were a little much for just two people. This was before her husband had shown up, and the fear that he eventually would come after her had Carrie insisting she stay in her rental, with its double locks and alarm system.

And I had promised my mother's ghost I wouldn't sell my childhood home.

But Mother had moved on...into the light, or wherever ghosts went, when they no longer felt tethered to the earth plane.

Then Phillip came into the picture, and the whole concept of cohabitation had been tabled indefinitely. Until he, Phillip, brought it up.

And already Carrie's talking about getting a house together?

My heart rate kicked up and my stomach felt kind of queasy. I probably should've grabbed some breakfast earlier.

I tried to steer my anxious thoughts elsewhere, and of course, they landed on Mary.

Was Carrie right? Had I stepped over the line from being a supportive friend to being a controlling jerk?

Mary had said she knew that wasn't my intention, but I didn't want to be a jerk, even unintentionally.

And bringing her to Virginia had been a mistake. It had brought her attacker down on all of us. What was I thinking? I shook my head slightly. It never occurred to me that her attacker was a full-blown stalker who would follow her wherever she went.

And what else could I have done? Insist she call the police?

I shook my head again.

Yeah, right. Insist a freaked-out rape victim call the police—I wasn't gonna do that.

"What?" Wallace said from the driver's seat.

"Nothing, I was just thinking."

"A dangerous activity sometimes," the sheriff quipped.

He was quiet again, and after a while I drifted into a light doze, my head leaning against the passenger window.

My skull bounced against the glass. "Ouch."

"Sorry, pothole," the sheriff said.

My head throbbing slightly, I looked around. We were in the city. I gave him directions to Mary's office.

"What should I call you while we're there?" I asked.

"Wallace will do. And I'd like you to organize things so I can talk to everybody today, assuming Mary's boss is cooperative."

"I...I thought we were both going to interview people?"

He glanced sideways at me. "I may be posing as a private eye but this is still official sheriff's department business. And we don't usually let civilians sit in on interviews with other witnesses."

Pressure in my chest. He'd set me up. "I need to know what's going on, if I'm going to keep everyone safe."

"I'll tell you anything pertinent." He glanced my way again. "And some folks would be intimidated by two interrogators in the room. Things'll go quicker if you locate people and bring them to me."

Begrudgingly, I nodded. "Why did you say if her boss cooperates? Why wouldn't Bevans cooperate?"

He shrugged. "Because he's a lawyer, and they are intrinsically suspicious and cautious, always worried about liability." He threw a hand up in the air in a disgusted gesture. "If they had their way, nobody would never do nothin', in case it brought a lawsuit down on 'em."

But Larry Bevans turned out to be totally cooperative. When I introduced the sheriff as a private investigator I'd hired to find Mary's attacker, he'd only asked one question. "So you don't believe Fred did it?"

I shook my head. "And neither does Mary. He's the wrong height and build, for one thing."

Bevans grimaced. "I'd hoped all this was resolved, for all our sakes." Then he offered a conference room for our use and called his Human Resources department, instructing them to give us whatever we needed.

The "department" was only one woman. She met us at her office door and shook our hands, introducing herself as Janice Freeman. She was dark-haired and petite.

After taking seats in front of her desk, the sheriff asked for a list of all the law firm's employees.

Ms. Freeman's eyebrows shot up. "We have twenty-four employees! Mr. Bevans's partner, three associate lawyers, their admin assistants, paralegals..."

Wallace had been nodding as she ticked them off. "We need them all. Is anybody absent today?"

She hesitated, then tapped on her keyboard. "One of the admins and the mailroom clerk."

"We'll need their home addresses," Wallace said.

She scowled at him.

"I can get a subpoena, if need be," he drawled.

"I thought you said you're a P.I., and didn't the police close the case on all this?"

Wallace leaned forward. "Keep this under your hat, okay? The detective on the case isn't totally satisfied. He'll be real happy if I can rule out anyone else, and he can rest assured that the culprit was indeed your young computer geek. But if it wasn't him, well, the detective will want to know that, too."

She was still frowning, but she gave us what we wanted. As she handed over the printouts she said, "Honestly, I don't think it was Fred."

"Whadaya mean?" Wallace asked.

"Oh, I can believe he had a crush on Mary. I'd seen him watching her walk down the hall with a puppy-dog look in his eyes. And maybe he'd kill himself over that unrequited love. But rape? And Mr. Bevans told me he supposedly shot at somebody who was looking into Mary's attack. No way." She glanced meaningfully at the large square plastic bandage that had replaced the white gauze on my bicep. "I'm assuming that was you who got shot?"

I nodded, opting not to get into the possibility that the shooter was after Avi, not me.

"What about the shooting bothers you, Ms. Freeman?" Wallace prompted her.

She shook her head slightly. "Fred hates guns." She paused, pursed her lips. "I shouldn't tell you this. It's supposed to be confidential." She took in a slow, deep breath.

Wallace sat patiently, waiting for her to continue.

"We're both in the same Al-Anon Family group," she finally said. "We grew up in alcoholic households. Both his parents were drunks, and they fought when they were sloshed, sometimes violently. One day, his father threatened his mother with a pistol. She got it away from him and shot him. Then, when she saw what she'd done, she shot herself." She paused, swallowed hard. "Fred was there. He was twelve."

My throat ached. I swallowed hard myself. Poor Fred. Then angry pressure filled my chest. Yet another reason to find Mary's attacker, who was probably also his assailant. Fred deserved justice too.

The interviews took between ten and thirty minutes—ten for the people who said they barely knew Mary or Fred. In such a small firm, you'd think they'd all interact regularly, but apparently Bevans's partner handled only corporate accounts, while Bevans was mostly a defense attorney. Their staffs operated fairly independent of each other, sharing only a few things, like the mail room, a receptionist, and Ms. Freeman, the HR lady.

We'd completed five interviews, when the next interviewee said he needed the men's room. Wallace and I waited in the hall, talking in low voices.

'What did you think of that story about Fred's parents?" I asked. "Does that weaken the case against him?"

"Maybe, maybe not," the sheriff said. "He might've hated guns, but that kinda background might make him pretty unstable, especially when it comes to relationships. And his role models for how to handle conflict weren't the greatest."

I nodded, just as my cell phone vibrated in my pocket.

"I wonder what that guy's doin' in there." Wallace started down the hallway toward the restrooms.

I pulled out my cell. The screen said *Carrie*. Dread filled my chest. Would she be mad that I'd slipped out without talking to her this morning? After last night, would she tell me we were through? My stomach roiled.

The sheriff's phone rang. He stopped and reached into his pocket.

I answered Carrie's call, faking a cheerful tone, "Hey sweetheart, what's up?"

Sobbing sounds. "James, oh my God..."

My heart went into overdrive. "What happened? Is Mary–"

"No, it's Phillip..." More sobbing.

A vague awareness of footsteps pounding toward me.

"What happened?" I yelled. "Is he hurt?"

Sheriff Wallace grabbed my arm, holding up his phone in his other hand. "We gotta go, son. My deputy says Carrie's boy's been kidnapped."

CHAPTER EIGHTEEN

Mary

We'd heard the car rumbling down the driveway and raced outside.

Now Carrie was sobbing, and my heart was breaking. I'd done this. I'd brought this down on my friends.

Chief Deputy Blanc had tried to convince me it could be a coincidence, or maybe Phillip ran away. But I didn't believe either of those lies.

Now Blanc was huddled with the sheriff, and James was trying to console Carrie.

I'm such a coward. I went inside.

I sat on the sofa in the otherwise bare living room. Ginger came up and placed her chin on my knee. I burst into tears.

I couldn't take this anymore. I wanted to rant and rave, tear my hair out by the roots, bang my head against the wall.

But I did none of those things, because I was timid little Mary. Instead, I sobbed into my hands.

My phone buzzed in my pocket. A text message.

I gulped down a sob, swiped my arm across my face, and pulled out my phone, tapped the icon for messages.

Only numbers where the caller's name should be. The message read: *I have Phillip. You for him, or he dies. I will*

*be in touch with details. You will come to me. If you tell ANY-
ONE about this text, he dies!*

Then the message disappeared. How could it do that?

—◆○◆—

Carrie

James was doing his damnedest to comfort me, his arms
around me. Through the fog of my anguish, that much
registered. I loved him for it.

But I couldn't say anything. My mouth felt like it was
locked shut. A sharp, intense ache filled my chest. I'd endured all those beatings at the hands of my late husband,
some came close to killing me—yet nothing compared to
this pain.

Oh, Philly! Memories flashed through my mind. Him as a
baby, barely two weeks old—the first time Greg had beat me
after his birth.

I shook my head, this wasn't about me, or the beatings.
Why did they keep intruding?

Awareness dawned. *Because I endured them to keep Philly
safe.*

And now after all that...after Greg was *dead*, for God's
sake...Phillip was not safe!

The sheriff was saying something to James, something
about finishing some interviews.

What the hell, why isn't he looking for my boy?

James stepped back. He patted my arm. "I need to talk to
the sheriff. I'll be right back."

An icy chill enveloped me as he withdrew his warmth.
And a deeper, older ache filled my chest and hollowed out
my stomach. An old familiar feeling of abandonment.

He was arguing that he should go with the sheriff, to finish interviewing some people in DC.

What the freakin' hell?

"No," Sheriff Wallace said, "you're not going this time. This is official. I can't have civilians..." He glanced my way. "Besides, you're needed here, son."

James turned back toward me. The anguish on his face made my heart squeeze. He felt awful too. He only wanted to *do* something, anything to find Phillip.

"This has got to be linked to all that's been happening with Mary," I said, as James returned to my side and slid an arm around my shoulders.

He nodded. "The problem is that the main suspects who might be her stalker and attacker are her coworkers. And the sheriff and I, we can confirm that the vast majority of them are alibied. They were at work when Phillip disappeared."

He cleared his throat and dropped his voice, "Um, I'm wondering why Annaleise didn't sound a warning."

My stomach roiled, and my cheeks heated with shame. "She did. The wind chimes were clattering when I turned off the sander."

James

I sat on the sofa of the otherwise empty living room. The room was cold, unfriendly. *Why hasn't Carrie used some of the proceeds from selling her ex's business to buy furniture?*

She had used some of that money to buy a new car, when Phillip had insisted—the money was technically his, as his father's sole heir. Most of it was stashed away for his college.

I'd helped things along regarding the car by pointing out that her clunker was becoming more and more unreliable. Phillip had insisted again, and she'd given in.

Her new car had all the bells and whistles—push-button ignition, a back-up camera, and other safety gizmos. I was a little jealous. I loved my classic Mustang, but its most modern feature was an FM radio, and the Bluetooth I'd retrofitted through that radio.

My mind decided it was done with my attempts at distraction. It veered back to the miserable evening we'd just endured.

Carrie was convinced it was all her fault, while Mary and I exchanged guilty looks. We both knew damned well it was ours.

"If only I hadn't decided to sand the porch today," Carrie'd said. "I should've realized the noise of the sander would cover any other sounds, like Ginger barking."

Another guilty look from Mary. "I heard her, as I was drifting off to sleep. I thought..." She paused, swallowed hard. "I'm not sure what I thought." She'd shaken her head.

Carrie had told the sheriff that she'd finished the sanding and came inside to clean up. That's when she'd realized Phillip wasn't in his room playing his video games, as he'd been doing when she went out front earlier. Of course, she'd left out the part about Annaleise's wind chimes alerting her, too late.

She'd searched the house, then roused Mary from her nap and the two of them had searched the property together. Safety in numbers, they'd figured.

They'd found Ginger in the backyard, lying forlornly by the gate. She was unharmed and the gate was closed, but the padlock was off.

I went over again what the sheriff had said. He and his deputies had searched the backyard and the field behind the house. They'd found some crushed down grasses that indicated someone had walked through the field recently, probably today.

But it hadn't rained in a while. The ground was hard and dry—no footprints.

Sheriff Wallace had also examined the gate and the lock. No signs of either being tampered with, so odds were good that Phillip opened the gate himself. But why would he do that?

"The FBI?" Carrie had asked.

"They're in the loop, ma'am," the sheriff said. "As is the Metro Police. Everybody's on the lookout for your boy."

Then he'd taken me aside. "We've asked the Feds to hold off jumpin' in on this. They don't have to unless he's taken across state lines. And we haven't sent out an Amber Alert. This guy, I doubt he's an experienced kidnapper. We don't want him to get spooked."

So the sheriff had instructed us in how to use the call trace feature on our phones, that would send any caller's info directly to law enforcement. And there now was a deputy inside the house, sitting at the kitchen table, an impassive expression on his face.

We'd anxiously waited all evening for a ransom call that never came.

Finally, I'd convinced Carrie to try to get some sleep. But I was too wound up to even lie down next to her.

My chest squeezed even tighter than it already was. I should be up there, comforting her. But I'd only keep her awake with my restlessness.

I laid down on the sofa, Carrie's pistol next to me, and crooked one arm over my eyes.

"Oh, Annaleise," I moaned. "I screwed all this up."

Wind chimes, faint and slow, almost mournful.

What am I going to do if we don't get him back safe?

The familiar warmth enveloped me—Annaleise giving me a ghostly hug.

But it didn't soak all the way in this time. My core remained cold as ice.

I was fond of Phillip. He was a great kid. My heart ached. I ground my teeth.

I'm worthless.

I couldn't protect Annaleise and Charles. I couldn't protect Phillip. And the bastard who was after Mary would probably get to her eventually, no matter what I did.

More warmth around me, that couldn't get in. The wind chimes now sounded like a dirge.

Mary

I sat on my small bed, fully clothed, head and torso propped against the wall. I had no intentions of sleeping. I was determined to do something helpful.

My laptop on my lap, I'd first looked up disappearing emails. Indeed, there was a way to make that happen. My inner nerd was tempted to research further, but I resisted the urge.

Then I'd accessed my office email account and was trying to find out who might have hacked into it, besides Fred.

No luck so far. I punched keys, trying a different approach.

An error message popped up on the screen. *This account has been locked due to suspicious activity.*

Damn it to hell!

I leaned my head back against the wall and blew out air.

I'd have to go to DC tomorrow and try again from my computer there.

My phone pinged on the nightstand. I grabbed it up—*4:20* the screen said.

My heart pounding, I opened messages. The same unknown number as earlier. The text read, *I have the boy. Pay close attention. Type yes to show me you got this.*

I'd barely sent my *yes* reply when the original message disappeared. I stared at the phone.

Another ping. *You for him. Come to me and I'll let him go.*

That text also faded after a few seconds.

Then another ping. *Get in your car and drive to the Capital Beltway. I'll tell you where to go from there.*

I jumped up, grabbed my purse, and realized with a jolt that I had no car here.

Panic quivered in my chest and made me queasy. I had to save Phillip, but how?

Another ping. *You have an hour and a half. Don't tell ANYONE.*

I stared at the message, trying to think. It too faded away.

I'd have to take James's car. I snuck out of my room and down the stairs.

He was asleep on the sofa, also fully clothed. And no doubt his car keys were in his pocket.

I slipped into the kitchen. The deputy and I both startled. I'd forgotten he was there.

"What–" he started to say.

I quickly put a finger to my lips, pointed toward the living room, then tilted my head, and held my hands together under my cheek, to indicate sleep.

I went to the sink, found a glass in the cabinet next to it, and poured myself some water. I gave a small finger wave at the deputy as I left the room, cupping that hand to palm Carrie's key fob from the small key rack next to the doorway.

I managed to tiptoe past James without waking him. There was a lamp on in one corner of the room. My guess was he hadn't intended to fall asleep down here.

No sign of Ginger. She was probably upstairs in Carrie's room.

I stood in front of the alarm box, trying to remember the code. Oh, yes, it was Phillip's birthdate. My chest ached.

He'd just had a birthday a few weeks ago...when was that? May? Yes, May tenth, and he'd turned fifteen. I did the math. 5-10-04.

I punched those numbers into the box. It emitted a low beep.

I winced and glanced over my shoulder. James rustled some, but his eyes were still closed.

I eased the door open, slipped out, and eased it closed behind me.

The front floodlights were on, showing the way to the cars. I raced for Carrie's, trying to find the unlock button on the key fob. I grabbed the driver's door handle and it opened. I almost fell on my keister.

I piled into the driver's seat, fumbling the key. It fell on the floor. Panic sent my already pounding heart into hyper-drive.

Wait, duh! I found the button on the dash and pushed it. The engine purred.

Not taking the time to put on my seatbelt, I backed around and raced up the driveway toward the road.

I glanced in the mirror. No lights behind me. I blew out air and relaxed a little.

Then it hit me—I was driving toward the man who'd raped me.

And once he had me under his control, he would no doubt do it again, and again. My hands trembled on the steering wheel.

But I kept driving.

CHAPTER NINETEEN

James

Wind chimes jolted me awake, plus I thought I'd heard another noise. I strained to listen. The faint crunch of tires on gravel.

I jumped up and ran to the front window, expecting to see a car coming toward the houses. But instead I saw taillights, moving away from me, fast.

And Carrie's car was missing from the parking area.

I turned and raced up the stairs, into the master bedroom, expecting to find it empty. But Carrie lay sleeping on her side of the bed, Ginger curled up beside her. The dog lifted her head.

Confused, but with a lump of dread in my stomach, I ran for Mary's room.

It was empty.

Heart pounding in my chest, I roared after Mary in my Mustang.

Why did she do this? I could make an educated guess.

She couldn't be that far ahead of me. But it had taken me a few minutes to shake loose from the house.

Carrie had come out of the bedroom, demanding to know why I was searching the upstairs.

"Mary's gone," I'd yelled as I rocketed down the steps, "in your car."

The deputy was in the living room, on his radio. He reached out a hand to stop me, but I ducked around him.

"Wait, Sheriff Wallace wants to talk to you." The deputy held out his hand, the radio in it.

"Tell him to call my cell in two minutes," I said, as I spotted the butt of the pistol sticking out below the front edge of the sofa. I must've knocked it onto the floor while I slept.

I'd grabbed it up and raced for the front door, the deputy trying to tackle me. But desperation was pumping adrenaline through my veins. I was too fast for him.

I'd jumped into my car and taken off, the deputy yelling something from the front porch behind me.

My phone rang via the retrofitted Bluetooth, but it had no caller ID screen. I answered, "That you, Sheriff?"

"What the hell're you up to, son?"

"Mary's gone. She took Carrie's car–"

"Yeah, I got all that from my deputy."

I think she's going to meet her rapist, to get him to let Phillip go."

"Did she leave a note?" he asked.

"I didn't see one."

"Well, you need to turn around and go home to Ms. Carrie. Me and my people will go after Mary."

"No! She's already got a bit of a head start on me. You'll be miles behind her. I have to catch up with her before she reaches the city."

"Are you sure that's where she's going?"

That brought me up short. "No, uh... I guess..."

"Does that fancy new car have LoJack?"

I sat up straighter in my driver's seat. "Yes, it does. Can you track it?"

"Probably. It'll take a few minutes to set up. In the meantime, I've got a couple deputies headed toward DC. I think you're right, that's the best bet. I'll alert the Metro Police as well, and the FBI. Now, go ho–"

"Keep me posted," I interrupted.

The sound of air being blown out. "You're not gonna go home, are ya, son?"

"Nope."

"Okay, let me know if you catch up with her," the sheriff said, in a resigned voice.

"*When* I catch up with her." I disconnected.

I was going as fast as I dared on the curvy country road. I should've caught sight of her taillights by now. What if I was wrong, and she hadn't turned toward DC?

There were dozens of farms and abandoned barns around here. She could be anywhere by now.

Dear God, don't let anything happen to her.

But I knew it wouldn't be good. She was walking right into a rapist's trap. What would he do to her, after...? Would he kill her?

I instructed my jury-rigged Bluetooth to call Mary's cell. It didn't always get things right, but this time it did. Only no one picked up. Three rings and it went to voicemail.

"Mary, where are you, damn it? And more importantly, where are you going? Call me, *please!*" I pressed the button to disconnect, then shoved the accelerator all the way to the floor.

A few minutes later, my phone rang. "Mary?"

"No, it's Avi. I can't reach Mary. Is everything okay?"

"No!" I shouted. I made myself pause and take a quick breath. "Nothing's okay." I filled him in on Phillip's kidnapping. A small voice in my head said I might be telling him what he already knew, if he was Mary's stalker/rapist. But then, why would it matter that I'd told him?

"I'm pretty sure Mary's going to trade herself for him," I blurted out.

"Oh my god! No!" A half beat of silence. "Where?"

"I don't know. Sheriff Wallace is setting things up to track her through LoJack. She's in Carrie's car."

"Okay, I'm getting in my car now, here in DC–"

"What about the trial? Isn't it today?"

"Last-minute plea bargain this morning. The producer's giving up the mob guys he worked for. I'm free as a bird. I was calling Mary to tell her..." He choked up a little.

Suddenly suspicious, I said, "You're calling this early?"

"She'd told me she was always up with the sun."

I looked around. A soft light now filtered through the trees along the roadside. It was indeed dawn.

I grunted.

"Let me know as soon as you have a location on Mary. Please, James–" His voice broke again.

I hesitated, then said, "On this number?"

"Yes. It's my regular cell phone."

I disconnected without committing one way or the other.

Once the sheriff let me know where Mary was headed, *should* I let Avi know?

Why not? If he was Mary's attacker, he already knew where she was going. And if he wasn't...

But do I want him rescuing her?

My chest tightened. Did I have to be the savior? What the hell was wrong with me?

It doesn't matter who saves her, as long as she is safe.

Then I thought about Phillip and my throat closed. Whatever went down between Mary and her attacker, his fate hung in the balance as well.

Wind chimes clattered in the distance, fading away completely as I got farther from home.

———◆———

Carrie

I couldn't remember the last time I'd felt this scared and helpless. Scared, yes, there'd been plenty of those moments in the last few months, especially when my abusive husband had shown up. But I'd had a security system, a noisy dog, and a gun. I hadn't felt totally helpless.

Now, I didn't even have a car. And I'd searched the house—my pistol was gone. Either James or Mary had taken it.

The deputy had refused to join the chase, to follow Mary and hope that she led to my son. He'd said he had specific orders from the sheriff to keep me here.

Damn men to hell. I was so sick of them trying to protect me, without even asking if I wanted that protection.

Okay, maybe that wasn't fair to the sheriff. I'd been more than happy when he offered to station a deputy here, until we got all this resolved.

"Lotta good that did us," I muttered. The stalker still snatched Phillip, and then lured Mary away. Heat flushed my face and upper body as I watched the useless deputy, standing in my living room.

"What was that, ma'am?" he asked, glancing my way.

Hot pressure built in my chest. It felt like it was going to explode. "I said, I'm tired of incompetent men telling me what to do, insisting on 'protecting me.'" I made air quotes.

Shame added to the angry heat in my cheeks. I knew I was taking my anger out on the wrong person, but I couldn't seem to help myself.

The deputy glanced over again. "I had the same orders regarding Mr. Fitzgerald, but he got past me, and I couldn't go after him without leaving you alone." He shrugged. "Ain't about male or female, ma'am. You're both civilians. It's our job to protect all of you."

Yeah, right. He wore that same stone-faced look I'd seen on the cops who'd answered the neighbors' calls when Greg was beating me.

I'd had to tell them I was okay, that I wasn't afraid of my husband, even though I was terrified. My eyes would beg them to see the real situation, that he would beat me even worse later, if I told them the truth.

With those neutral cop faces, they'd ask if I wanted to go to a shelter. And when I'd shaken my head, they'd told me there was nothing they could do if I wasn't willing to cooperate.

How I'd wanted to cooperate with them, but they couldn't protect me 24/7 and anything less than that....

I shook my head now, trying to ward off the memories.

The deputy was still staring at me from across the living room.

I wanted to rant at him, yell obscenities, tell him how worthless he was. But I made myself turn on my heel and march into Phillip's room.

I also wanted to throw myself on my son's bed and give in to the sobs that were clamoring to get out. But I didn't do that either. I was afraid if I started crying, I'd never stop.

I sat down on his desk chair and stared around the room, trying to imagine my Philly was here, chatting with me.

It didn't work. My mind kept conjuring up images of my baby, tied up and gagged, in some dark, lonely place. My heart ached.

And the room felt emptier than the living room, even though it was crowded with his things. The guitar and lacrosse stick leaning in one corner, plus other teenage-boy paraphernalia that we'd gone back to the Connecticut house to retrieve, before I'd put it on the market.

The plan was to use the proceeds from that sale as a down payment on a house near Paxtonburg. I sighed.

Opting to pretend that all would be well—Phillip would be found safe and sound and we would be moving by the end of the summer—I decided to distract myself with a real estate search.

I turned to Phillip's computer, and a notepad next to his keyboard caught my eye.

The word *Suspects* was underlined twice, above a list of two names.

———◆———

James

Halfway to DC, my phone rang again.

"Hello?" I answered hesitantly, thinking I really needed to figure out how to rig a caller ID to the Bluetooth. I usually just picked up my phone to look at the screen, but at the speed I was going right now I needed both hands on the wheel.

"James, I found something." Carrie's voice, semi-frantic. "Some notes by Phillip's computer, so I checked his browser history. He did a rudimentary background check on every person in Mary's law firm. And then he dug deeper into some of them–"

I interrupted. "Anything that indicates someone lured him out of the house?'

A half-beat of silence. "No, nothing like that. At least, not that I could find. But he has two suspects. One is the mail room clerk, a Carlson Daniels."

"He'd called in sick yesterday," I said. "I don't know if the sheriff caught up with him or not."

"Well, he's a small-time marijuana dealer on the side, and Phillip found a connection between him and that Fred guy, the one who committed suicide–"

"I don't think he did," I said.

Another pause. "Did what?"

"Commit suicide."

"That's beside the point," she said, her voice now impatient. "They were apparently friends. What if Fred gave this Carlson kid info on Mary, and that's what he meant about feeling guilty because he'd hurt her."

I opened my mouth to again deny the authenticity of the suicide message on Fred's computer monitor. Then thought better of it. "Yeah, I guess that could be."

I swallowed hard, feeling more than a little overwhelmed. Here I was racing down this curvy country road, trying to rescue her son and Mary, and I had to worry about not hurting Carrie's feelings when she floats a lame theory about the mail room clerk.

"Okay, I'll call the sheriff with that info. I gotta go, focus on my driving."

"Wait, James! There's one other person on Phillip's suspect list."

When she told me the identity of that person, I almost drove off the road.

Then she told me the rest of what Phillip had found.

CHAPTER TWENTY

James

I'd thought Carrie's theory—well, Phillip's to begin with—was shaky, but the sheriff had confirmed that Mary seemed to be going toward that section of DC. After warning me again not to go in alone, he'd disconnected to contact the FBI and the Metro Police.

Now, I was hesitating before placing my next call. I sighed and gave the Bluetooth its instructions.

Avi picked up on the first ring. "James, did you hear anything?" He sounded as desperate as I was feeling.

Somehow that desperation was reassuring.

"Where are you?" I asked.

"In my car, outside my apartment building. I realized, after I talked to you before, that I had no idea where to go. No point in wandering around town aimlessly."

"I'm almost to DC, and we think Mary might be going to an abandoned industrial park, but we're not one-hundred percent sure."

"What's the address?" The sound of an engine starting.

I gave it to him, then said, "Phillip had done some online research that Carrie stumbled on. Mary's boss's law partner, Peter Dawson, bought two warehouses in that park a couple of years ago. The LoJack indicates that Mary's headed that way."

I paused, sucked in air. "And get this—she and Dawson went to the same high school, although Mary was a year behind him."

"That's a bit of a coincidence," Avi said.

"Yeah. Sheriff Wallace pointed out that law enforcement folks don't really believe in coincidences."

"So maybe this Dawson guy has been obsessed with her for a long time?"

"That's what the sheriff's thinking. Dawson ducked him yesterday, when Wallace went back to finish the interviews. Said he was late for a meeting out of the office and couldn't talk."

I paused, debating about the next part. "The sheriff told me to tell *you* to keep a low profile." Actually, Wallace didn't know that I was passing info on to Avi. He would not have liked the idea one bit. *I* was the one he'd instructed to keep a low profile.

"Just cruise around and see if you can spot her car, until the police get there." I gave him a description of Carrie's car.

"Are you planning on waiting for the police," Avi asked, "if you get there first?"

I didn't say anything.

"That's what I thought," Avi said. "Don't worry, I'll be careful. I don't want to spook whoever it is."

He disconnected, and I rehashed what else the sheriff had said. The mail clerk was in the wind. He hadn't shown up for work again today, and he wasn't at his apartment. The Metro Police had been watching it, waiting for him to come home.

So, both of Phillip's theories had some merit. I felt a strange mixture of pride, worry, and a vaguely uneasy feeling. Was Phillip a full-blown hacker?

Mary

I'd parked Carrie's car behind the old warehouse, as the accented voice on my phone had instructed. I didn't recognize it nor could I pinpoint the accent.

"What now?" I said.

"Go in the door," the voice said, "to the right of the second loading dock."

I pocketed my phone and got out of the car. But now that I was here, full-blown terror was kicking in. If I thought the man in that warehouse was only going to kill me, that I could face. But I was turning myself over to a rapist.

My heart pounded in my chest, and my knees were like jelly. With difficulty, I walked slowly to the designated door, gripped its handle.

I gave it a tentative tug. Yes, it was unlocked.

And I froze there, unable to move. My stomach roiled.

Then my mind flashed to a scene from a few weeks ago when I'd been visiting James and Carrie, before....

Phillip had been playing with Ginger in the backyard. Carrie was watching them from the back door, a small smile on her face.

I took a deep breath, pulled the door open, and hesitantly stepped inside.

It took a moment for my eyes to adjust to the dark shadows of the empty warehouse. Despite the June heat outside, it was dank and musty in here.

A large lump, a darker shadow, rested near a wall, roughly fifteen feet from me. I took two steps toward it, squinting, trying to make out what it was.

The shadow coalesced into a person, sitting on a chair, arms tied behind their back, something across their mouth.

Phillip's eyes, full of fear, met mine.

"Ah, there's the *sheila* now."

I whirled toward the voice.

James

I gnashed my teeth at the city traffic, which normally didn't bother me.

But there were way too many law-abiding citizens out today, doing the speed limit—or less, in the case of the jackass in front of me who seemed to be looking for a parking space.

He found one, began to parallel park, and I veered around him. Horns blasted. I ignored them as my phone buzzed.

"Best we can tell," Wallace said without preamble. "She's in that industrial park. And her phone just pinged off a nearby cell tower."

I stomped the accelerator down and pounded the heel of my hand on my horn.

"James, stop!" the sheriff yelled from the Bluetooth speaker. "Wait for the police and the FBI! They're three minutes out, and I'm less than ten minutes away."

Three minutes! Two people I loved could be hurt, or worse, in three minutes.

I disconnected from the call.

My phone pinged on the passenger seat. A text coming in. The retrofitted Bluetooth couldn't deal with text messages.

I took the risk and picked the phone up to read the message.

———◦———

Mary

"Let Phillip go," I said, trying to sound firm. But there was a distinct quaver in my voice. "You have me now."

"No can do," the guy said. "I'm only the hired help."

I squinted down the length of the warehouse. Windows, high along one wall, let in some daylight. A man stood about thirty feet away, in one of the squares of light. He was solidly built, his feet planted slightly apart. A gun in one hand, raised toward us.

He was no taller than me, and he'd called me *sheila*. Was he Australian?

Definitely *not* my rapist.

As he'd said, just the hired help. He wore dark clothing and had something covering his nose and mouth.

A flash of movement behind him. I tried not to react.

Maybe I'd imagined it. I'd been praying all along that someone would show up to rescue us—even as I was hiding my car on a side road not far from the house and letting James's Mustang fly on by. Then I'd taken back roads to the Capital Beltway and raced around to this side of the city.

Now fear for James, or whoever it was, did battle with hope inside my chest. My stomach churned.

Another movement. I hadn't imagined it!

Someone stepped into the square of light, less than ten feet behind the guy with the gun, and slowly walked toward him.

Avi! I let out a gasp.

A sharp pain shafted through my heart. My attacker had been Avi all along.

CHAPTER TWENTY-ONE

Mary

Aussie Voice whirled around, arm raised.

Another figure jumped from the shadows and took Avi down, just as a shot rang out.

James? The glimpse I'd gotten was someone tall and lean. Or was Avi here to save me and the rapist had tackled him?

Confused and panicky, I looked around. Did the shot come from Aussie Voice? Or was there someone else with a gun in here? James would've brought Carrie's pistol.

My gaze landed on Phillip. He was slumped over in his chair. I screamed and ran for him. "Phillip!"

"Stand still, chickie," Aussie Voice said.

I ignored him.

I reached Phillip and my hands quickly explored his upper body. His left shoulder was sticky with hot liquid, and he was unconscious.

Had the bullet hit his heart? I ripped at his shirt, exposed the wound, put pressure on it with the heel of my hand, hoping to stop the bleeding.

"Leave him be, Mary." A voice from behind me. My stomach hollowed out.

I knew that voice all too well.

I turned my head, keeping my hand on the wound.

My boss, Larry Bevans, smiled at me, a large pistol in his hand. "Don't worry, we'll call an ambulance once we're out of here."

"What about me?" the accented voice said.

"I've got your money," Larry growled. "But what the hell were you doing, shooting at me?"

"I thought you was someone else."

Larry let out a disgusted grunt. He gestured at me with his pistol. "Come on, Mary. The sooner we get on the road, the sooner help will come for Phillip. I've been stashing money in a Cayman account for a while. We're going to live in paradise."

He gave me a smile that turned my stomach.

I stood and stepped between the two armed men and the boy. My heart was pounding, my brain whirling. I couldn't think straight, but one thing I was sure of, I wouldn't let them hurt Phillip again.

Even if it meant going with a rapist. I took a step toward him.

"Freeze!" Another voice I knew well.

Larry jerked around, pointed his gun toward the other end of the warehouse.

I glanced at Aussie Voice. He was on the ground, wrestling with someone.

Avi?

A roar deafened me.

I twisted and threw myself over Phillip. He groaned from beneath me.

He's alive!

———◆———

James

I sat in the hospital waiting room, elbows on knees, my face in my hands. I was trying to wrap my brain around the fact that I'd shot a man. And that he might die. He was in surgery now, but he'd lost a lot of blood.

A man I knew, at that.

If it had been the masked stranger I'd shot—the man Avi had jumped and taken down—would that have been easier to deal with?

But that guy had quickly realized he was outnumbered when the warehouse was overrun with law enforcement—the Metro police and FBI, with Sheriff Wallace and his deputies right behind. "Don't shoot me," the guy had yelled. From his prone position under Avi's weight, he'd scooted his gun across the floor.

I closed my eyes and felt again my pistol jerking up when I'd pulled the trigger, and Bevans had crumpled to the ground. I shuddered.

Then I flashed to Phillip's unconscious body, coming out of that warehouse on a gurney. Throat tight, I realized I would pull that trigger again, if need be, to protect the boy.

And Phillip was okay; everyone I loved was going to be okay.

Phillip's wound had been caused by a ricochet. It had gone in on an angle, away from his heart, and out the back of his shoulder. Lots of blood and some soft tissue damage, but his doctor predicted a full recovery.

The sheriff had told the deputy guarding Carrie to bring her to DC. She had barely given me a glance as she'd rushed by, on her way to the emergency room. Was she mad at me, or only in a hurry to make sure her baby was okay?

Avi had a concussion—his head had hit the concrete when I'd tackled him.

Thank God he'd texted that he was going in. Otherwise, I might have hesitated, and he would've been shot by Larry's henchman before I got there. I'd seen the guy starting to turn and instinctively threw myself at Avi to get him out of the line of fire.

And thankfully he hadn't been knocked out. I'm not sure what would've happened if I'd been up against Bevans and his hired gun alone.

Avi was clutching the sides of his head as we'd scrambled into a dark corner of the warehouse. There he'd whispered, "I'll sneak up on the guy. You get Mary and the boy out of here."

He'd probably thought he was volunteering for the more dangerous task. But things had not gone as planned, after Larry Bevans showed up.

Avi's doctors were fairly sure there would be no long-term damage. Mary was with him now.

Or maybe she wasn't. I'd caught a whiff of roses, her signature scent, as clothing rustled beside me.

Mary.

Great detective work, I sneered at myself inside my head. I shook off the self-flagellation and sat up. "Hey, Mare, how're you doing?"

"Okay, I guess."

"Avi okay?"

"Yes. He fell asleep, so I figured I'd check on you."

"Shouldn't he be staying awake?" I said.

Mary gave me a small smile. "The nurses said that's been debunked, that sleep is a good thing. It will help his brain heal. So, how are you doing?"

"Okay." But I realized I was shaking my head.

Mary frowned. "No, how are you, *really?*"

I took a deep breath. "I'm struggling some with the fact that I shot a man, maybe..." I trailed off.

"You had no choice. He was going to shoot you, and then maybe finish off Phillip. Not to mention what he would have done to me."

I could feel her trembling, where our arms touched.

I wrapped an arm around her shoulders. "Yeah, my head knows all that, but it's still hard."

She nodded and slipped her arm around my waist. She squeezed and let go, moving slightly away from me.

I let my arm drop and swallowed a sigh. It might be a while before she'd be totally comfortable with touch again.

After a moment, she shook her head. "It's surreal. I've wished my attacker dead many times, even fantasized about how I would kill him, if I got the chance. And I don't think I would have felt bad afterwards. Not after what he did to me. And what he's put all of us through."

She shook her head again. "But when I think of him as Larry, my boss—the man I worked for, all those years. We spent many a late evening working on cases, and..."

"Never a hint?"

She shrugged. "He asked me out a couple of times, after Nick and I broke up. I told him it was too soon. But I also had concerns about dating my boss. He dropped it after the second invitation. Looking back, he began to get more touchy-feely after that. That hug outside the building the other day, that wasn't a total surprise."

"His obsession was secretly festering inside of him."

She gave me another feeble smile. "Rather dramatically phrased, but yes."

I rolled my eyes. Annaleise had teased me about being dramatic. Apparently, Mary was taking up that dropped gauntlet.

"When I think of him as my boss," Mary continued, "I want to cry for him. I can't believe he'll never walk through the law firm's doors again." She choked up a little, then cleared her throat. "I guess it will take some time to adjust to the idea that he was also my attacker."

My phone pinged. I pulled it out of my pocket. It was a text from the sheriff. *Figured you deserved to know this...*

I smiled grimly. "Maybe this will help with that adjustment. Sheriff says the tracks up on the road, where I almost hit that car, they match the tires on Larry's Audi."

Mary's eyes had gone wide. She nodded, her lips a thin, straight line.

"I wonder what set him off," I said.

"The Friday before, I mentioned something about having a big date over the weekend. He asked a few questions, like anyone might, and told me to have a good time." She sighed. "But I suspect he'd been stalking me for a while. I ran into him around town quite often, and now I'm thinking that wasn't just chance. And he probably hacked into my office email long before last weekend."

"Have you heard anything about Fred?" I was almost afraid to ask.

"Yes." Mary's face brightened some. "I talked to his sister. He's in a medically induced coma, but the doctors...well, they aren't totally pessimistic. The question is how much brain damage there will be when he wakes up."

I suspected that was the best we could hope for, at this point. *Poor Fred.* My chest felt heavy.

"Fred's not your fault either," Mary said. "This is all on Larry."

Okay, Miss Carry-the-Weight-of-the-World, I thought but resisted saying out loud.

Instead, I gave her a small smile. "The sheriff told me Metro Police is now investigating his fall as suspicious. His doctor told them the head injury was more consistent with being hit by an object than from a fall, especially onto grass."

"So Larry must've hit him, then shoved him out the window. He was covering his tracks–"

"And using Fred as a scapegoat," I said.

"Wait." Mary furrowed her forehead and turned a little to face me. "How did Larry show up at the same time, out front? He couldn't be in two places at once."

I shook my head. "I thought at the time that Fred probably hadn't fallen right then. Some of the blood was already drying on the grass."

She winced. "He'd pushed him out the window earlier, then pretended he was coming back from a tennis game."

"I wonder," I said, "what would've happened if the sheriff and I hadn't shown up asking questions yesterday. If Larry had thought he'd gotten away with blaming everything on Fred."

Mary's lips were pressed together in a grim line. "I doubt he would have given up. He would've just waited for me to let my guard down."

My stomach clenched. I consciously relaxed it—that hadn't happened. "Are you going back to work at the firm?"

"I guess. But I think I'll ask to work for Peter Dawson instead, in corporate law. I can't imagine working criminal cases with some other boss. If Peter even keeps the criminal side of the firm going."

"Speaking of Dawson, he was the one we'd suspected, because he knew you from high school and owned the warehouse. Do you think he knew Bevans was using it to hold Phillip?"

Mary shook her head. "No, he bought it and another one last year. Then his investors backed out, and his plans to renovate the whole park and rent out the warehouses fell apart. He's been trying to figure out what to do with those buildings since then. He's even talked about donating them to a charity."

"You didn't recognize the address?" I asked.

She shook her head again. "I never knew it before. I only know that much about Peter's attempt at real estate development from one of his paralegals. She'd mentioned it once over lunch. And by the way, I got the job originally because Peter knew me from high school."

I chuckled softly. "So sometimes coincidences have logical explanations. We thought maybe he'd been obsessed with you for years."

"Ha," Mary mock laughed. "He's engaged to a model."

I was thinking that talking about Dawson and his warehouses had distracted her from more intensely charged thoughts, when her shoulders began to shake. She let out a low sob.

I wrapped my arms around her, pulled her to my chest.

My throat tightened. "Shh, shh," I whispered. "It's okay. It's over."

One more heaving sob and Mary pulled away. She blew out a long sigh. "Thanks, I needed that."

She smiled up at me, eyes shining through residual tears. "I think that was as much about relief as anything. The nightmare really is over, isn't it?"

————— ◆ —————

Carrie

James had tried to talk both me and Mary into going home. We'd both refused.

Finally, at one in the morning, he convinced me to take a break. Mary promised to stay with Phillip, who was sound asleep—as was Avi, in a room five doors down. The doctors had insisted on keeping him overnight for observation.

James and I got soup and coffee in the hospital cafeteria. There were just a few medical folks, wearing scrubs in various colors, scattered about the tables.

We carried our trays to a far corner and ate in silence for a couple of minutes. I was having trouble choking the broth and vegetables down. My stomach was still tense and queasy from all the worrying.

James cleared his throat. "Are you mad at me for abandoning you at the house and taking off after Mary?"

I sighed. "I *was* furious, but now... Honestly, I don't have the emotional energy to be mad."

"I'm sorry. I really didn't have time to think it through. My vague plan was to catch up with her, then circle back to get you. I thought I'd catch her within a mile or two of the house. She said she hid on a side road and waited for me to go by."

I scooped up another spoonful of broth but didn't bring it to my mouth.

James ate some of his soup. "Did Phillip tell you how Bevans got his hands on him?"

My stomach clenched even tighter. I let the broth dribble back into my bowl. "He said it wasn't Bevans, it was that other guy. Phillip was in the backyard, checking your makeshift alarm system by the fence. Ginger started barking, and a male voice yelled over the fence to open the gate."

I paused, my chest tightening as I imagined the scene. It was getting hard to breathe. "Philly swears he checked the guy out, through the crack between the gate and the fence. He was too short to be Mary's attacker, and the guy told him he was our landlord. Ginger wouldn't stop barking so Phillip slipped out of the gate, closing her in the yard. He was going to bring the guy around front to me. The guy grabbed him. Phillip got out one yell—which was drowned out by the sander."

Guilt squeezed my heart. "Then the guy slapped a hand over his mouth and dragged him across the field out back, and stuffed him in the trunk of a car."

James had put down his spoon. He blew out air. "That's one tough kid."

"He's tough because he's had to be tough," I said, my tone sharper than I'd intended.

James nodded slowly, his expression sad. "I know."

Then his eyes went wide. "Wait! That guy obviously wasn't wearing anything over his face out by the fence, or Phillip never would've opened the gate."

My stomach roiled as the implication sank in. "They'd never planned to let him go."

"No, but the guy covered his face in front of Mary, because they *were* going to let her live." He paused. "Although Bevans wasn't planning on ever letting her go, so he didn't care if she saw his face."

We both shuddered. After a beat, James picked up his spoon again.

I broke off a piece of roll and dipped it in my bowl. My eyes on the soggy bread, I said, "What would you have done if you'd caught up with Mary? Would you have hauled her back to the house to keep her safe?"

I knew it was a loaded question, but I had to know. Would he have left Phillip to die in order to protect his friend?

James shook his head. "No, I would've gone to the warehouse with her and tried to rescue Phillip."

My stomach relaxed some. I brought the broth-soaked bread to my mouth. Its warmth was soothing as it slid down my throat.

"Did you have a plan?" I asked.

He grimaced. "Not really. It was kinda hard to think while going a hundred miles an hour on a country road. Plus the sheriff kept calling with updates on the LoJack, and each time, he'd remind me to wait for the police if I got to her first." He looked up, met my eyes. "I wasn't sure I could make myself do that."

"Well, you didn't." My voice was a little terse. "You went in before he got there." I couldn't help wondering if Phillip would have been spared a gunshot wound if James had waited.

"Mary and Avi had already gone in," James said, "so whatever confrontation was going to happen had already begun. And again," he paused, swallowed hard, "I didn't have much time to think."

I half-snorted. "What is it they say, about fools rushing in?"

"Okay, what would you have done?" His tone was terse now.

I opened my mouth, then closed it again. Was I being unfair? What *would* I have done?

I gave him a chagrined look. "I probably would've rushed in there too."

He let out a low chuckle and ate a chunk of roll.

My stomach rumbled, now relaxed enough to feel hunger. I greedily spooned up soup.

"I've been giving what we talked about a lot of thought," James said.

"Which topic?" I asked. "We've talked about a lot of things lately."

"Well," he said, in a low voice, "let's start with the topic we're already on. Do I have a savior complex? Yeah, I probably do. Am I fighting it? Most definitely. Am I trying to control anyone? I don't think so. Am I going to stop protecting the people I love?" He paused, sucked in air. "I think the answer to that one is *hell, no.*"

He held my gaze. I put down my spoon.

"I don't think I *can* stop," he said. "I get this sense of urgency and I've got to act, to do *something*. And I realized today, as I was racing down that road, it's the same feeling I had the day Annaleise... the day I found them, her and Charles. I was telling myself there had to be something I could do, if I could just get help there fast enough, maybe they'd be okay."

He shook his head. I reached over and took his hand.

He grasped mine tightly. "I knew they were gone, but..."

"Sounds like the denial of grief to me," I said gently.

"Yeah, of course..." He trailed off again, looked away, blinking. "But now, when there's any chance at all that someone may be okay, if I act fast enough. It's like a compulsion."

"That makes sense." I covered our clenched hands with my other one.

I lifted my eyes to meet his. If it was true-confession time, then I should admit... "I've been giving the whole issue of protection and control some thought as well. I've always associated control with abuse, from my mother, and then from Greg. But after the last two days... Well, I'm now feeling this intense urge to lock Phillip in his room, at least until he's eighteen. I won't, but it's what I want to do. To keep him safe."

I blew out a sigh. "So I'm getting it that protectiveness can morph into control, out of love. And that control doesn't always lead to abuse."

He gave me a lopsided grin. "Well, I'm hoping life will settle down now for a while, and we won't need to worry about protecting anybody. We've had more than enough evil show up in our lives this past year."

"Yes, we have." I paused. "So, what else were you thinking about?"

"The moving thing. I think I've gotten used to the idea. We need a new place that's *ours*. My house has too many bad associations now. And yours, well it isn't yours."

"We could buy it, if you want to stay out there in the country."

"No, not really. I don't really want to be *in* town, but closer to it and the high school would be fine."

I squeezed his hand. "You know we need to do something about Annaleise, before you sell your house. We can't just leave her there."

"No, I know that. But I'm not sure how we get her to let go."

I squeezed again. "I think you *both* need to figure out how to do that."

———◦———

James

The thought of never hearing those wind chimes again made my stomach queasy. I pushed aside my soup bowl and opened my mouth.

Movement across the cafeteria caught my eye. Mary was headed our way, her face bright and smiling.

"Phillip's awake," she said as she got closer, "and he's asking for you, Carrie."

Carrie let go of my hand and jumped up. I began to follow suit.

"Stay and finish your food," she ordered in her Mom voice.

"Now who's being controlling?" I said.

Her face fell.

"I'm only kidding." I chuckled. "Go to Phillip. I'll bus our dishes and be right behind you."

———◦———

Mary

I went to Avi's room to check on him. A nurse was there, taking his vitals.

After she left, he patted the side of his bed. "Come here, Beautiful."

I smiled, suddenly feeling shy. "You're looking pretty fine yourself," I said.

"Yeah, sure. Doing a face-plant on a cement floor was bound to improve my features."

We laughed together and my shyness dissipated. I sat on the edge of the bed.

"Mary, I've been thinking." He waved a hand in the air. "All this—having to go into hiding, meeting you, then almost losing you. It's made me realize that we shouldn't be wasting one moment of our lives."

He stopped, took a deep breath. "I know I've acted like a bit of an ass, kind of love-bombing you...and I know it's too soon. But, um, sometime in the not too distant future, I'm going to ask you to marry me. I just thought you ought to know that."

My heart swelled but I managed to keep my face blank. "You're right," I said.

His expression turned wary. "About which part?"

"It is too soon. After all, we've only ever kissed once." I gave him a mock glare.

"Well, that is easily remedied." He took my hand and tugged on it.

I hesitated, then lowered myself beside him, laying outside the covers. Anxious butterflies had invaded my stomach. Would kissing Avi trigger flashbacks?

He stroked my cheek, gazing into my eyes. "I lov–"

I quickly put my finger on his lips. "No, it's too soon for that too. Just. Kiss. Me." I tried to laugh but it sounded more like a nervous giggle.

He smiled slightly and did just that. A gentle chaste kiss. *No flashbacks!*

I felt my muscles relaxing, for the first time in days.

EPILOGUE

Carrie

In early August, it was still hot and humid even after dark. Tomorrow, James, Phillip, and I were moving to our new house, three miles outside of the town of Paxtonburg.

But tonight we had unfinished business.

Phillip thought we'd gone out to dinner—we'd left him happily playing his video games in his room. But we were actually gathered in the woods, about a hundred feet behind James's garage. Where it was unlikely that Phillip would notice the small bonfire we had going.

Mary was there, and Avi had also insisted on attending. James had designated him as the watcher, one who would stand aside, not participate, but would be there to help if anyone needed assistance.

I wasn't quite sure what that meant, but I trusted James. He'd spent hours online, researching various approaches to helping a trapped soul depart from the Earth plane.

I also wasn't quite sure I believed in all this stuff, but I did know two things. Annaleise's ghost was real, and she needed to move on. I was hoping that whatever mumbo-jumbo ceremony had come out of James's research would help her do that.

He had some sage burning slowly in a small bowl. He passed the bowl up and down in front of each of us, even Avi. Then he walked around behind us and repeated the process.

A gentle breeze swirled the fragrant smoke around me. I closed my eyes, and as James had instructed, told myself to let all negative energy flow out of my body.

James put the bowl down on a large rock and picked up a small set of wind chimes. He'd gotten several at the dollar store and had passed them out to each of us earlier—not including Avi that time.

He gently shook his now. Mary and I followed suit.

"Annaleise, are you here?" he asked. "Can you hear us?"

Her wind chimes answered him, slow and solemn.

She knows what's coming. That thought surprised me.

Then I realized it shouldn't. She'd no doubt listened in on our many discussions, maybe even hovered over James's shoulder while he was researching on the computer.

James nodded at Mary. "I'd like you to go first, like we talked about."

Looking nervous, she stepped forward, closer to the fire. "Annaleise, you were the best girlfriend I ever had. If you hadn't been there when Nick and I separated..." She choked up, swayed a little on her feet.

Avi moved to just behind her and put a steadying hand on her shoulder.

She gave him a small smile and cleared her throat. "Thank you for staying with us for so long, Annaleise. We will miss you, more than you can imagine, but it's time to go." She paused. "Go be with Charles. He must miss you terribly."

The firelight gleamed off Mary's wet cheeks as she stepped back, Avi beside her.

James nodded at me. The skeptic in me wanted to roll my eyes, but I squashed the temptation and stepped forward.

"Annaleise, I never knew you before... But I've heard about you, a lot." I hesitated, not sure what to say next.

Then the words seemed to come to me. "I know that you loved your friends with all your heart. Indeed..." I felt my own heart expanding in my chest. Wind chimes tinkled softly. "I think maybe you are the most loving person I've ever known." I let out a nervous snort. "Or known about, in this case."

I paused, took a deep breath. "Thank you for taking good care of James, and for looking out for me and Phillip." My heart swelled again at the memory of her warning me when Greg was nearby. "But we're going to take care of each other now, so you can move on."

More tinkling of wind chimes. A warmth encircled me, like a gentle hug.

A teardrop landed on the front of my blouse. I swiped at my wet cheeks and, on shaky legs, stepped back.

James stepped forward, gently rattled his small wind chimes, and closed his eyes. Seconds ticked by. He didn't say a word.

Then a smile spread across his face. "That's an excellent idea," he said out loud.

He opened his eyes and stepped over in front of me, his face now serious. He took my hands, a bit clumsily since we both still held our wind chimes. "I know we both have issues, and sometimes they feed into each other. But as long as we're paying attention, working hard not to let them trip us up..." He trailed off.

I nodded, not sure where he was going with all that.

"Annaleise just whispered two words, and I agree with her." Grinning, he dropped down on one knee. "She said, *marry her*. So... Carrie Peterson, will you marry me?"

My heart felt like it might explode. I suspected the sensation was not only from my own joy, since wind chimes were clattering like wedding bells.

I strained to push past the feelings and think it through. Yes, my mind agreed with my heart. It was time. "Yes, I'll marry you."

James jumped up, grabbed me and held me tight. The wind chimes sang out. Mary ran over and wrapped her arms around both of us.

I glanced at Avi, a few feet away. He had an indulgent smile on his face.

A warmth enveloped us, lingered for a few seconds. Then it and the wind chimes slowly faded away.

I broke the hug and looked up at James. "She's gone." I choked a little on the words, which surprised me.

"I know," he said, a soft smile on his face, even though his eyes were shiny.

Avi stepped over and laid an arm around Mary's shoulders. She looked up at him, her expression soft, loving.

"Annaleise whispered something else," James said in a low voice, "as the warmth was fading."

"What?" Mary and I asked in unison.

"'All of you, just *be happy*, damn it.'"

Mary laughed. "That is so Annaleise."

AUTHOR'S NOTES

If you enjoyed this story, please check out my other offerings at the *misterio press* website (https://misteriopress/authors2/JessicaDale.com). This is Book 3 in this trilogy. Book 1 is *Payback*, and Book 2 is *Backlash*.

Also, reviews are always appreciated! You can find the links to leave one at your favorite book retailer at https://misteriopress/bookstore/backfire.com.

We at *misterio press* take pride in putting out stories that are as free of errors as possible; therefore each of them is proofread multiple times by several people. But proofreaders are human. If you found any errors in this story, please email us at kass@kassandralamb.com so that they can be corrected. Thanks so much!

Much gratitude to my beta readers and my critique partners at *misterio press*, all of whom gave invaluable feedback that made this story better. Also a big thank you to my husband who is my final proofreader.

This is the final book in the James and Carrie trilogy, and it's kind of hard to let them go.

Twice in my twelve-year writing career, I have woken up in the morning with a story pretty much completely written inside my head. Not just a story idea, but the whole thing.

The first time was the story of James being suspected of Annaleise and Charles's deaths. I wrote and published that as a stand-alone horror story/mystery for that Halloween.

Then a couple of years later, the story of *Binding Choice* appeared in my head one morning, full blown. I was actually a little shocked, since this was a very steamy and dark romantic suspense, not at all like the cozy/traditional mysteries that I had been writing up to that point.

But I couldn't *not* write it. The story wouldn't leave me alone. Once it was down on paper, I had to make some decisions: to publish it or not, and if I did, under what name. A new pseudonym seemed appropriate, so Jessica Dale was born.

Then I got an idea to rewrite the James story as a romantic suspense, giving him a love interest and a character arc in which he struggles with intimacy issues.

After that first story, I had to write the rest of the trilogy the old-fashioned way. Come up with a story idea, flesh it out a bit with a rough outline of plot points, and then sit down and see where the characters took me. It been so much fun seeing how they have evolved over the course of these three books.

This last book was perhaps the most challenging. In the previous stories, Mary had been painted as a passive, fragile creature with brilliant computer skills. A handy sidekick to help James solve the mysteries.

Now I had to flesh her out and give her a character arc in which she could come into her own. It took several drafts and a good bit of input from my wonderful critique partners at *misterio press* to finally get there. But I am pleased with the outcome.

I hope you are as well.

ABOUT THE AUTHOR

Jessica Dale is the alter ego of mystery writer, Kassandra Lamb.

Kassandra has always been passionate about two things, psychology and writing, and she also loves new challenges. After a successful career as a psychotherapist and college professor, she retired and started writing fiction, primarily mysteries.

Several years later, when she'd accumulated several plot ideas for romantic suspense stories, she decided it was time to branch out. And since some of those stories were rather steamy, a new pen name seemed to be in order.

Thus, Jessica Dale was born. In addition to those steamier stories, she wrote the Unintended Consequences trilogy. These stories are sweet romance, but there is plenty of suspense and edge-of-your-seat excitement in them.

Readers can connect with Jessica via her alter ego at https://kassandralamb.com. Also, you can sign up there for their newsletter to receive a heads-up when there are new releases, plus several free stories!

Kass/Jessica's email is kass@kassandralamb.com, and they both love hearing from readers!

Please check out these other great *misterio press* series:
Karma's A Bitch: Pet Psychic Mysteries
by Shannon Esposito
Multiple Motives: Kate Huntington Mysteries
by Kassandra Lamb
The Alchemical Detective: Riga Hayworth Paranormal
Mysteries
by Kirsten Weiss
Dangerous and Unseemly: Concordia Wells Historical
Mysteries
by K.B. Owen
Murder, Honey: Carol Sabala Mysteries
by Vinnie Hansen
Full Mortality: Nikki Latrelle Mysteries
by Sasscer Hill
Payback: Unintended Consequences Romantic Suspense
by Jessica Dale
Buried in the Dark: Frankie O'Farrell Mysteries
by Shannon Esposito
To Kill A Labrador: Marcia Banks and Buddy Cozy
Mysteries
by Kassandra Lamb
Lethal Assumptions: C.o.P. on the Scene Mysteries
by Kassandra Lamb
Never Sleep: Chronicles of a Lady Detective Historical
Mysteries
by K.B. Owen
Bound: Witches of Doyle Cozy Mysteries
by Kirsten Weiss
At Wits' End: Doyle Cozy Mysteries
by Kirsten Weiss

Steeped In Murder: Tea and Tarot Mysteries
by Kirsten Weiss
Steam and Sensibility: Sensibility Grey Steampunk
Mysteries
by Kirsten Weiss
The Perfectly Proper Paranormal Museum Mysteries
by Kirsten Weiss
Big Shot: Big Murder Mysteries
by Kirsten Weiss
Plus even more great mysteries/thrillers in the *misterio press* bookstore.